I0537771

Kinky Girls Do

An erotic short story collection by
Michelle Houston

MICHELLE HOUSTON

www.unleashedink.com

KINKY GIRLS DO

This book is dedicated to all the girls who grew up hearing "good girls don't do that!"

Stay safe, practice sane ... and always, always ... it must be consensual.

It goes without saying that in any writing endeavor, there are those that are behind the scenes that make writing possible. To all who have assisted me along the way - thank you.

A special note of appreciate to D. Musgrave and Jenna Brynes for hours of editing and critiquing, as well as friendship.

And to my husband - who supports me even when my characters scare him a little bit - my heartfelt thanks and love. Without him, these stories would never have been written.

TABLE OF CONTENTS:

YOUR ATTENTION PLEASE

There was no way around it, Angela was an attention slut. Shaking her tits in guys faces, and letting them slip money into her g-string got her hotter than Nevada in July. The loud, throbbing music always got her going, as it washed over and through her. She selected her music carefully, knowing just what would allow her to show off her body in the best light.

As she watched Bethany, a new girl, stumble up the steps behind the stage to observe her act, Angela tossed her a knowing smile. "Relax, kid. You'll knock them dead."

Bethany smiled shyly in response. She was kind of cute. "I'm not sure that I can do this."

Unfortunately, she was definitely too timid. "You know ballet, right?" Angela continued at Bethany's nod. "Then you already know how to captivate an audience. That'll give you an edge. Just remember, they're here to watch you, not the other way around. They're paying to see your body, so you own them. Use them and walk away. Make them want more. It's what I do."

"...And now, here's our luscious Chantal, for her last set of the night." The voice of the DJ echoed throughout the back room.

"That's my cue." With a flirtatious wave, Angela pushed through the curtains and stepped onto the stage.

9

As it always did, the light blinded her for a moment. It was the perfect time for a dramatic pause. She could feel the gaze of the audience as if it were a living entity, caressing all over her body; they would be admiring her assets, their minds comparing her to the girls who had gone on before.

She knew the picture she posed: long blonde hair, slim waist and very ample breasts. As her eyes adjusted to the lights, she strutted out onto the stage. With each step her peek-a-boo lace gown tightened against her torso, the trimming brushing against her thighs. A line from *Pretty Woman* always ran through her mind: "Work it, girl. Work it, work it." That's what she always tried to do.

Across the room, Darren stood waiting, as he did every night she danced. Their gazes met, and she tossed him a smile before looking away. A shiver raced down her spine, as she moved across the stage. She could feel his gaze following her as he leaned up against the wall, his muscular arms folded across his broad chest.

Looking out at the audience, she focused her attention on a spot just above their heads as she danced around the stage. Dropping to her knees, she occasionally spread her legs, a special treat for those who were seated close to the stage.

There was an art to stripping that many never seemed to master. It wasn't about flawless movements and all the fancy shit that you see in the movies. Although she loved *Flashdance*, she knew what a disservice it did to many strippers. The audience for the most part doesn't care about the theatrics. They want to see tits and ass. And it's the strippers' job to give it to them.

The song ended and another began, flowing almost seamlessly together. The DJ and Angela had worked together long enough to get the music for her set perfected. As the beat slowed slightly, she lifted her hands to the waist of her gown, pausing seductively. Hoots and hollers came from the audience. Egged on, she untied the ribbon that held the bottom half of her gown closed. Grabbing the edges she pulled it open and turned her back, looking coyly over her shoulder. They were eating it up. Tonight was definitely going to be a lucrative night.

She flipped the skirt up over her ass, showing off her barely there thong. Giving a shimmy, she rolled her hips, drawing attention to the shapely curves of her ass. As she bent over, baring the firm globes, she could feel her thong tightening, the thin strip of her g-string parting her ass-cheeks. As she stood upright, she slid her hands up her body, caressing her legs and sides.

Spinning around, she looked out at the audience as she did a hip rotation, judging their mood and what was catching their attention the most. Each audience was different, and she had learned to play up to what worked with each. Lifting her hands to her hair, she let the tresses slowly fall between them, fluttering around her face and shoulders.

Again their gazes met, and even from across the room Angela could see the fire in Darren's eyes. He appeared calm and collected, but she knew the beast within him was tightly leashed, waiting to spring free. She shuddered at the delicious knowledge of what was to come.

Grabbing the pole, Angela spun around it, her thong pulling tightly against her pussy. As soon as her heels touched the stage, she bent over and shook her ass, watching for cues from between her legs. Spotting a bill being waved at her, she stood up, running her hands up the back of her legs and over her ass. Pivoting on one foot, Angela strutted across the stage and crouched. The five slipped into her garter. Smiling at the balding man who gingerly brushed the back of his hand against her skin, she leaned forward, her lace-covered breasts a breath from his face. His eyes almost crossed and she smiled. She loved this. Despite making a good living, it was the attention that made stripping perfect for her.

11

Dropping back onto her hands, she thrust her barely covered crotch into the balding man's face. Eyes wide, he slipped another bill into her garter. As he moved back, Angela gracefully flipped herself upright, grateful as always for years of martial arts training.

Spotting her stool on the corner of the stage, she worked her way to it and pulled it to the center, while dancing around it and subtly loosening the ties on the top half of her gown. Climbing up, she hooked her feet around the legs, grabbed the back of the set, and arched. Breasts straining against the lace covering them, she wiggled to loosen the ties, and then relaxed, dropping back to a normal sitting posture.

Parting her legs, while leaving her feet still anchored, she ran a hand over her body, and treading on thin ice, she rubbed it over her crotch, just enough to tempt but not enough to push the obscenity laws and get the club fined.

Pumping her hips, she gave allusions to masturbating, and then allowed her hand to drop to the stool.

Curling her fingers over the hard wood, she arched again, feeling the gown burst open, baring her whole body to the audience's view. Sliding carefully and with a sinuous grace off of the stool, she caught her lace confection between her body and the edge of the stool and slid free of it. Shifting to her knees, she tossed gracefully towards the back of the stage, and crawled to the front edge.

She could feel her pulse racing. Adrenaline surged through her as her gaze flicked across the room again to meet Darren's. His lips curved into a shape with which she was intimately familiar. She was pushing all his buttons. The animal within him was breaking free and she was to be dinner. She would have purred if she could.

The second song ended and slipped right into the third. Hard, pulsating music blasted over the sound system. The deep bass pounded into her. Her pussy clenched in need. Four minutes to go and she would head backstage. Four more minutes, and he would be there

12

waiting for her. She would be his. But now, her audience demanded her attention.

Reaching her destination, she stood and caressed her body, her hands running lightly over her stomach down to the band of her thong and pulled the material up into the wet folds of her pussy. Angela's lips parted for the delicate lace, allowing it to slide against her throbbing clit. Those close to the stage could see her juices glistening on her inner thighs.

Several people held up money, eager to catch a glimpse of her pussy up close. Stepping over to them, the thin material rubbing deliciously between her lips, Angela crouched down. Those putting money into her garter could smell her sweat and essence combining into a musky tang all her own. One daring woman leaned forward, her clothing brushing against Angela's leg, as she slid a bill into the thin strap of the g-string that curved around her hip. The woman's nostrils flared as she inhaled deeply, before she moved back.

Angela moved around the edge of the stage as the music was drawing to an end, the last minute winding down. As subtly as she could, she moved the money from her thong to her garter, as more money was added. The audience was slowly losing her focus, no longer holding her attention as much as Darren did. His gaze was steady on her, mesmerizing.

His arms were no longer folded across his chest. Instead, he held his hands fisted at his sides. Angela knew if it was quiet in the room that she would be able to hear his growling, the deep sound welling from the dominant side of his nature. He was finished allowing other men to ogle her. Why he insisted on watching her last set of the night, when he knew it would get his desire all worked up, she didn't know. And frankly, given the pounding he would give her later, Angela didn't care.

As the last bars of the song crashed over her, she moved to the center of the stage and dropped to her knees. Arching back to her shoulders, she grabbed the edge of her g-string and pulled it hard, snapping the thin fabric. For a brief moment, she bared every inch of her body to her audience, as the last beat of the song echoed against the walls of the bar. The lights above the stage went dark.

Dropping to lie flat, Angela took a few deep breaths, and then rolled over and stood. Her legs a little shaky after the fifteen minutes of non-stop mental foreplay, she quickly grabbed her outfit and stool, and stepped off the back of the stage, into the back room, and moved aside as the next dancer's name was called.

Lily paused at the edge of the curtain. Swatting her ass, Angela told her to knock 'em dead. The first song of the next girl's set started, and she stepped onto the stage.

Angela watched Bethany for a moment, smiling as she stared hypnotized at Lily's antics on stage. Gently, Angela clasped her shoulder in her hand and whispered in her ear, "Just remember, it's all about you."

She nodded shakily and Angela turned away to grab her robe off the back of a nearby chair and hurried to the dressing room. Several of the women were back there, chattering as they took their break, but they all knew she wasn't interested in pausing to wind down.

With sly smiles, lots of winks and comments while she hurriedly dressed, they bid her goodnight.

Grabbing her purse from her locker, she rushed out of the back room. Pushing through side door, Angela exited the building into the parking lot. There Darren was, waiting for her. His dark-eyed gaze trailed over her as she moved towards him, his hot eyes fairly burning through her clothes. He turned the key and started the engine on his bike as she moved to stand beside him. She climbed on behind him and wrapped her arms around his waist, holding tight to his muscular body.

Her breasts crushed against his back as he guided the machine out of the parking lot and into the busy traffic.

The vibration of the motorcycle was working its way through her system. Angela loved it when the night was clear and he could pick her up this way, rather than in his car. She knew she would be dripping wet by the time he peeled her jeans down her legs.

Wind rushed past them, whipping through her blonde hair, as he effortlessly guided them down the street and around corners. Time no longer had meaning, what seemed only a heartbeat later, they pulled into the parking lot of his apartment complex.

After pulling into his slot, he slid down the kickstand and killed the engine. Angela sat behind him, her breath coming in little gasps from the exhilaration of the ride. It was the best way to wind down from a night at work.

"Come here," Darren rasped the first words he had spoken all evening. Lifting her foot, she wrapped it around him, and with his help, slid around in his lap, so that she was facing him. All around them, apartments faced the parking lot. Any one of his neighbors could be watching them, but she didn't care. It was all part of the rush.

Threading her fingers through his hair, Angela pulled his head down to hers. With a growl, his lips pressed against hers, his tongue sweeping past to claim her mouth. His arms tightened around her waist, crushing her against his chest.

Her hands slid down to his shoulders, gripping them as she leaned back, breaking the kiss. His lips moved to her neck, and he bit her. She knew that he was claiming her, marking her as his in the most elemental way. In his way. Shivering at the delicious sting, she ground her crotch against the hard bulge of his lap. His hands cupped her ass and he stood. Swinging his leg over the bike, he climbed off. Angela unlocked her legs from around his waist, and slowly slid down his body. When her feet touched the ground, the top of her head barely reached his chin.

It always made her feel fragile, standing against him. Despite her years of martial arts training, she knew if it came down to it, he could easily overpower her. Yet he never made her feel threatened, just... conquered. Even now, when she could feel the effort it took for him to hold himself still rather than throw her to the ground and thrust into her, she felt safe.

As she stepped back, the street light cast half of his face in shadows. The other half seemed chiseled from stone, with its strong jaw line and sharp cheekbone. Clasping his hand in hers she led the way to his apartment, making sure to add a little sway to her walk.

A delicious tingle worked down her spine as she mounted the steps, slowly moving closer to her destiny. She was going to be fucked. Judging by the way he had looked at her in the club as she had danced, it would be hard and hot as hell.

When they arrived at his door, he reached around her and unlocked it, pushing it open for her. Angela stepped into the dark hallway, and the instant the door closed, he was on her. His arms slid around her waist and held her trapped against him. She could feel his hot breath against her neck as he fought for control. "I want you," he breathed.

Almost frantically she worked at the buttons of her jeans. Bending over, her ass rubbing teasingly against his groin, she slid her jeans and panties down her hips and kicked them off. Turning in his arms, she reached for the buttons on his shirt and worked them free; pressing little kisses against his chest as she slowly bared his smooth skin.

He didn't show as much restraint with her shirt. He raised his hands, grasped the edges of the fabric, and pulled, popping the buttons off. They hit the wooden floor with tiny little pings. Then his mouth was on her, his teeth rasping against her breasts as he tugged at the edge of her bra.

As Darren yanked the material down, Angela's left nipple sprang free. Nipping at the hard bud, his hands clasped her hips and pulled her tight against him. His zipper rubbed against her clit, generating a sweetly painful friction. Arching against him, she teased herself against him as she reached behind her and tugged at the clasp on her bra. Sliding her arms free, Angela let it fall to the floor.

Darren's hands cupped her ass and pulled her up against him. Wrapping her arms around his neck, she climbed into his embrace. But instead of carrying her to the bedroom, he moved over to the sliding glass doors that lead to his balcony.

He set her down in front of the doors and stepped away. "Wait here," Darren ground out, his voice deep with need. Then he stepped away. In the near dark, with moon light behind her, she couldn't see what he was doing until he flicked on a light beside the sofa.

He was breathtaking standing there in the dim light, completely naked, his cock sheathed in Latex. As he moved towards her, her heart started to pound. He moved like a panther, slowly creeping up on its prey before pouncing. Then he was there, a breath away from her.

Suddenly, he gripped her hips and spun her around, pressing his body against her back. Holding her hips, he guided her to lean against the door. "You're a cock tease, and you know it, right?"

"Mmmhmm," Angela murmured.

"And you love it. Showing off your body, getting men all hard and horny, then leaving them wanting you."

"Yes." She knew what he was doing, and she craved it. She could feel her juices trickling down her thighs

Darren hand gripped her hair tightly, pulling her head back. "But you're not going to get away with it Angela. Tease."

His other hand tightened its hold on her hip, pulling her back into the curve of his hips. His cock slid along the cleft, brushing against her pussy lips. Reaching down, Angela parted them and gently guided his cock head in, then reached up to hold onto the door.

17

MICHELLE HOUSTON

"Fucking cock tease." That was all the warning she got before he thrust hard against her, driving halfway in. Angela braced herself against the door as Darren pounded against her. "Say it."

"I'm a cock tease," she gasped, as his cock filled her.

"Look out the glass. Out there any number of men could be watching you get fucked, pretending it was them instead of me fucking you."

"Yes." Just the idea made her hotter.

"They're stroking their dicks, imaging your tight cunt wrapped around them." Angela imagined there were dozens of gazes watching them from the other apartments; hands slowly stroking cocks as he thrust against her.

His teeth nipped at her neck as he pounded against her. Her pussy clenched around him, tight with the steady build up of sensations that welled within her. Angela leaned against the doors, her nipples tingling with the contact to the cold glass. She shuddered in his arms.

"You purposely teased me tonight, driving me slowly out of my mind, watching other men watch you."

"Mmmmhuh." Darren's hand tightened in her hair, and she arched her neck back, giving him greater access to the slender column of muscle he loved to bite.

"But you're mine." He bit down as his cock surged into her. She wasn't sure how much more she could stand. Her orgasm was building with her, tightening all of her slick inner muscles. "Mine to fuck."

"Yes." She whimpered in need. She knew he could hear her, but he continued his steady even pace.

"You're mine. Say it." She could hear his harsh breathing in her ear and feel the heat of his breath on her shoulder. The masculine pitch of sounds that was distinct to him.

"I'm yours." And that's all it took to unleash his animal. With a soft growl, he surged against her, his hips slamming into her ass cheeks. Her arms shook as she

18

braced herself. His hand untangled from her blond tresses and joined hers on the glass, bracing them as he pulled her into each of his thrusts.

She closed her eyes as a riot of sensations crashed in her body. The whirlwind twirled inside of her, centering within her pussy. He thrust hard against Angela, raising her onto her toes and her world exploded. Her pussy clenched tight around him, milking his cock as tiny rushes of pleasure washed over her.

Her legs threatened to fold under the weight of his onslaught, but his hand on her hip held her up as his cock swelled inside her. He ground against her, his hips making tiny jerks against her as he came.

When her pulse calmed, and she could breathe again, she opened her eyes and looked out into the night. Across the parking lot a light flicked on, and she saw one of his neighbors standing there, watching them.

"We have an audience," she whispered. Behind her, he fought for breath, his body trembling.

"Good. Let them watch. They can't have you."

Pushing off from the glass, she turned in his arms and wrapped her arms around his neck. He grabbed the cord and pulled his blinds closed.

* * *

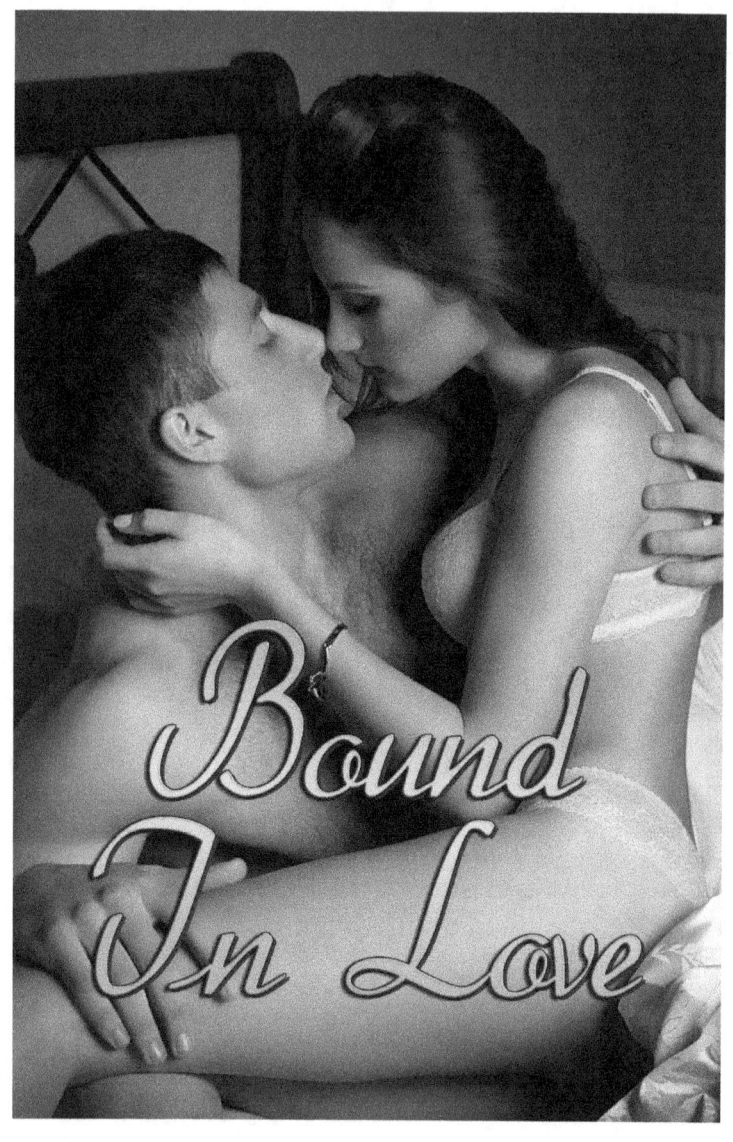

Bound In Love

BOUND IN LOVE

Yvette leaned back against the plush leather seat and sighed deeply. "I don't know what to do, Doctor. I know he loves me, and I trust him. I just feel kind of nervous about him tying me up. How sad is that? I've been married almost four years to Brett, but sometimes I still have flashbacks and nightmares. Yet, I admit, the idea of being helpless, his to do with as he wills," Yvette's voice trailed off as she struggled to put to words the feelings that were welling up.

Ever since Brett's latest tour started, each time he got leave, things had slowly been evolving in the bedroom. He had completely stopped pulling her down on top of him during sex; instead he was the one in control. His grip on her hips was just a little tighter, his touch a little rougher.

From across the room, her therapist met her gaze with steady gray eyes. "Does it turn you on, thinking about it? Him binding your hands, and being free to touch you however he wants?"

Yvette gave a little jerky nod. She had to struggle to resist the urge to squirm in her seat. Just the very thought of Brett dominating her was enough to start her juices flowing in preparation for his cock.

"Does he know you were raped?"

Her voice a soft whisper, Yvette answered, "No. It's never come up. I don't know if I can tell him."

"What you're feeling is natural—the fear and the excitement. After the trauma of your rape, it's normal for you to feel hesitant with trying things that take away your control. But you and I both know that you would be doing yourself a disadvantage if you deny yourself something you find exciting, especially with someone you trust."

"I know." Hearing the hesitancy in her own voice only hardened Yvette's wavering resolve.

"How do I—" She paused, licking her suddenly dry lips, trying to frame the question in her mind. "How do I let him know to go slow without telling him what happened to me?"

"Would telling him be so bad?"

Yvette gave a shaky nod. She needed her therapist to understand. "When he looks at me, he sees someone who's got it together. He sees me as I was before the rape. And for the most part I do too. But some things still make me flinch, my stomach gets all tied up in knots, and I hate that my rapist still has that power. I am not a victim. But if I tell him—"

She felt the sting as tears formed in her eyes. Blinking rapidly to keep them from falling, she forced herself to rush on. "If I tell him, he'll treat me different, like a bird with a broken wing. I'm afraid he'll smother me, keeping me from having the independence I've struggled to regain. I know he won't do it on purpose; it'll be out of love." She took a breath to calm her jagged nerves, "I can't tell him that while he was stationed overseas, fighting to keep me and this country safe, someone attacked me."

Looking into those gray eyes, Yvette felt a soothing energy flow over her. That's what she liked about this therapist, her third since the attack. She listened, didn't push or judge, and she had the deepest gaze full of understanding. It allowed Yvette the time to heal at her own pace.

"Since he returned, has sex been as it was before the rape?"

"Sort of. He's only been back twice for a week's leave. Things started changing in the bedroom about two years ago, almost a year before the rape. He started getting a little more intense. He touches me so gently, like he always has, yet now it's a little rougher. His hands hold me tighter. He's strong, and he knows it, so he's still careful with me. Plus, with him being over a foot taller than me, and let's face it, I'm a 110-pound weakling, he's always so aware of his strength."

Yvette curled her legs up and rested her chin on her knees. "It makes me shiver just thinking about it, the ways things had been changing. Looking at him across the table at dinner, knowing the leashed animal magnetism, and the beast of lust that lurks within him is enough to get me hot. Doctor, it's what first drew me to him, the way he filled out his uniform as he walked down the street, so confident in himself and his abilities. This last two years, it just got better, until," her voice broke off again.

A few moments of awkward silence filled the room as Yvette struggled to continue, and found herself unable to.

"How do you feel about it now, when he touches you? When he's covering your body, driving into you?"

Yvette fought the flinch. "I love him. I trust him, and I try to not remember what happened. I tell myself that the rape had nothing to do with sex, it was all about power. With Brett, it's about power to some degree, but it is more about love and feeling close to each other, being intimate on the most basic levels."

"But sometimes…" She knew she was being led, but the soft voice only encouraged her to open up.

"Sometimes, especially when's he's really horny, he pins me to a wall, trapping me. I get a little light headed for a moment, but it feels so good. His strength, his love, his body pressed against mine. God Doc, I used to love it so much when he'd chase me around the house, sometimes out into the yard, and pin me down and slowly make love to me, holding me trapped beneath him." She paused, trying vainly to remain calm. "So I'm sick. Is that what you wanted to hear? I had rape fantasies before I was raped." She could hear the defensiveness to her words, but couldn't stop it.

Unperturbed, her therapist leaned forward, her voice still as calm and even as before. "First, Yvette, you're not sick. There's a difference between forced seduction, or even a need to submit sexually, which is what you have with your husband, and what that sick monster did when he raped you. Secondly, it is healthy to have fantasies and to explore them. Him tying you up and making love to you, claiming your body in an intense seduction is healthy. Especially given his career field, him being able to control you sexually, to feel your response to his dominance over you, is something he probably needs too."

Yvette nodded, feeling shaky but beginning to understand what her therapist was trying to get to. "So what I want with him is forced seduction?"

Her therapist nodded. "Exactly. Just like many of the romance novels out on the market, where the heroine wants the hero, but either likes to be coerced or simply feels secure enough to give in to the need to submit. Rape is where she has no power in the situation, where it is forced upon her with no way out. It's completely different, in forced seduction or even sexual submission there is an illusion of control that your husband has, but it all rests with *you*. With your husband, all you have to do is say no, and I am sure he will pull back. Ultimately, you hold all of the power."

Yvette nodded. "Yes," she whispered. "When we first started playing with spanking, it got too intense, and I told him to stop. He did, and then spent the next twenty minutes kissing every red spot on my ass. It was delicious, almost more so than the spanking. I loved laying there over his lap, letting him kiss and caress me. One of his hands rested on the small of my back, holding me still."

The session continued for another twenty minutes and by the end of it Yvette felt rung out, but also relieved. It had taken some doing, but she thought she was ready for when her husband got home on leave in two days. She was going to explore their fantasy, and at the same time, discover if she truly was a sexual submissive. After the last few sessions with her therapist, Yvette was coming to see that Brett had been holding back—and so had she.

* * *

Two days later, she was dressed in a lace gown over a set of pink underwear, waiting by the door when she heard the taxi cab pull up. The sound of heavy boots thumping on the porch announced him moments before the door swung open. As was their custom, he tossed his bag on the floor, swept her into his arms, and kicked the door shut, holding her tight against his chest while he plundered her mouth with his.

Returning the kiss with all the pent up passion in her tiny frame, Yvette wrapped her arms around his neck and let him carry her to the bedroom.

Every time he came home for leave, the homecoming was always bittersweet. None more so that this one. Now, he was stationed stateside again—his tour overseas at an end. He might have to be gone for a few weeks at a time for training, but it would be nothing like going six plus months without him.

"Damn, baby, I missed you," he growled against her neck while kissing the slender muscle. As they reached the bedroom, he gently laid her on the bed and moved back to trail his gaze over her. "Have you missed me?"

Yvette smiled, her pulse already racing in response to her answer. Playing their game, she leaned back on her elbows and purred, "I guess I have. Although with work and all, I really didn't notice the time flying by."

After his first six week stint for training, they had started playing this game that it didn't matter. It tore Brett up thinking about her alone, missing him, aching for him while he was gone. But his sense of duty demanded he stay with the military and serve his country in its time of need, despite his own views on where it took him.

"Mmm, good. We kept busy, too, playing poker at night and getting in lots of sun tanning during the day."

Yvette's heart clenched at his words, but she struggled to not let it show. Every day had been torture, struggling to not turn on the TV and sit fixated, waiting for news of the area of the world he was stationed in.

Reminding herself of her earlier promise, she sat up and slowly pulled off the lace gown, revealing the dainty pink bra and panty set to his hungry gaze. "I have to admit, though, I've been very bad."

Brett arched an eyebrow at the change to their routine, but bless him, he played along. "Oh?"

"Mmm, yeah." She arched her back, pushing her breasts against the lace bra covering them, her nipples hard and aching for his lips. "I ran through three eight-packs of batteries while you were gone. My poor pussy got so sore from the workout, but I couldn't stop."

Brett knelt on the bed, his large frame hovering over her as he leaned down.

"Yeah?"

"Yes," she hissed, her body on fire with need. Deciding to take the plunge, she took a deep breath and taunted him. "I think I need to be tied up tonight, so I can't touch it while you have your way with me."

A blaze formed in his brown eyes. Without warning, he pounced. Grabbing his belt, he whipped it out of its loops and loomed over her, pushing her flat onto her back.

"You have been a bad girl, Yvette. I don't mind you playing a bit, but that's my pussy you've abused."

Yvette shivered in sensual anticipation as he wrapped the leather around her wrists and pulled it through the buckle, then pulled her arms above her head. As he started to wrap the leather around the bedpost and tie it into a complicated knot, she involuntarily jerked. She could feel a trace of panic rising within her. She didn't know if she was ready for this, but as his gaze met hers, so full of love and desire, she fought against the fear. The panic wasn't enough to take her breath away. Not yet anyways.

As he moved back and stripped off his clothing, baring the magnificent body that was half-genetics and half-military training, she felt her pussy clench. She licked her lips as she watched the play of muscles as he moved over her. His hands, rough with calluses, caressed her legs as he pulled them apart and up, draping them over his shoulders.

Pressing soft kisses against her panty-clad crotch, he crooned softly, "Poor little pussy. She didn't take good care of you, did she? It's okay baby, daddy's home now."

Yvette arched her hips, anxious to feel the flick of his tongue against her clit.

His head whipped up and his gaze pierced into her, full of heat. "Enough. You abused my poor baby; I have to take care of her first."

Pulling at the leather wrapped around her wrists, the buckle scraping against her tender flesh, Yvette couldn't pull free, and Brett was obviously planning to torment her. Unable to break her bonds, she lay there, panting after her exertion while Brett continued to softly blow on the panties covering her pussy, the damp material clinging to her skin.

"Brett," she gasped as he nipped at her puffy lips.

The glint in his eyes gripped her as he lifted his head to silently scold her. Slowly, he shifted his body, a panther stalking its prey, moving with a sinuous grace as he held her legs clasped over his shoulders, pinning them against her chest.

She was helpless, unable to move. Just like that time. She closed her eyes, fighting the instinctive panic, knowing if she gave in, that would be it. She'd have to tell Brett what had happened.

As the blackness of her secret threatened to overwhelm her, Yvette's eyes flared open and started into Brett's brown gaze, seeing it full of love and desire. Matching her breath to his, she was able to fight through the panic and revel in the thrill of being tied up, helpless to his passion.

"Damn, baby, I've dreamed of this so many times. In the desert heat, at night, when all was calm, I'd fist myself imagining you laying there, your hands bound as I slowly fucked you." His cock pressed against her pussy, his hips rotating in a sensual grind against her. "Or it would be daylight, and I'd chase you across the dunes and when I caught you, I'd tie you up and slowly thrust into your wetness."

She could almost see and feel it. His tall frame bending over her, her smaller body pressed between the warmth of the sand and the warmth of him.

He surged against her, and she bit her lip, holding back the words that were forming. She wanted to beg him to take her, but knew he'd only prolong the teasing if she did.

Her knees brushed against her breasts as he pressed down harder, his body pinning her as he ripped the thin panties from her. The sound echoed in her memories. His warm gaze had become her lifeline, holding her to the present, keeping her from the painful remembrance.

They had made love several times since her rape, in the two weeks he had been on leave, but she had had always had a way to wiggle away from him. Now, there was no escape, she had no control or power.

Rather than terrify her, she could feel her essence leaking from her pussy, her inner thighs wet with her own juices.

"Do you want me?" he taunted, brushing his cock against her outer lips.

Yvette nodded her head.

"Say it," He growled.

She loved the husky rasp to his voice, the tightly leashed need dripping from his abrupt demand. She knew she needed to say it as much for herself as for him.

The choice needed to be hers. She realized that it was true what her therapist had said; despite being bound, she was still in control. Brett's reasoning had always been that with his size, anytime he had the advantage, which was almost always, he needed to pause. It was just one of the things she loved about him. He had had her pinned against a wall before, his cock pressed tight against her crotch, and he had held there for what seemed an eternity until she had demanded he quit teasing her.

"Fuck me," she rasped, her throat tight with need.

Brett shifted again, his cock nudging at her entrance. "Mmm, baby, I could stay like this all night." He slipped just an inch in, and then wiggled his hips. Her clit on fire with need, Yvette tried to shift beneath him, but her position held her almost immobile.

"Brett, please," she whimpered, needing him to claim her, to replace the horror of the rape with a new memory.

Brett's eyes were her lifeline, she held his gaze as he thrust hard, driving his cock deep within her. Tightening her legs as they lay over his shoulders, she squeezed her inner muscles tight, trying to hold him inside her.

With a smile of pure masculine satisfaction, Brett slipped free, withdrawing until only his cock-head was within her.

She tried to pull her arms down to pull him in, but couldn't move. The buckle of the belt scraped the back of her hand, only heightening the moment as she squirmed, trying to coax him deeper. His chest hair tickling her breasts, she whimpered her need, unable to speak for the riot of emotions clouding her thoughts. She was afraid of just what she would say, so she held silent.

His eyes lit with a fire, he moved slowly, thrusting into her, holding his body from crushing her. Immobilized, she could only lay there, waiting with anticipation for the down-stroke, and trying not to gasp in dismay as he pulled back.

Her legs had long since gone numb and become useless, lying limp over his shoulders as he pumped his cock in and out, the sheer strength of his body amazing to her.

Yvette could feel her body building to an orgasm, her pussy clamping on him like a vice.

"That's it, baby," he groaned, sensitive to the least little flutter of her muscles. She knew he could feel her legs tightening, the muscles rippling along his arms. Each flutter of her pussy had to feel like the sweetest of caresses along his cock.

"Come for me. You're mine, Yvette. Mine, baby."

"Yes!" she agreed.

Pumping hard, his body jostling hers, Brett worked them both to euphoria. Wrapping her hands around the remaining length of the leather belt, she hung on tight as she reveled in the force of his thrusts. She could feel his heart racing against her inner thigh.

Unable to move, she couldn't shift away from the approaching orgasm; all she could do was welcome it. Closing her eyes, she tightened her body around his and reveled in the explosion of sensation as her other senses compensated. As the rush descended upon her, every nerve ending feeling like a current of low volt electricity was pouring into it, she screamed out his name. Thrashing her head from side to side, one of the few movements she could make, she let the climax enfold her, holding her within its sweet embrace.

She could dimly hear Brett's harsh groan before he dropped his head to the pillow next to hers, always carefully to hold his body up. The strain on her legs suddenly went away as he rolled to her side. With a soft moan, she stretched out, her toes curling as the last wisps of pleasure slipped away. Opening her eyes, she watched his arms shake with the force of his climax.

As his eyelids flickered open, and he turned his head so that his gaze met hers, a lazy grin crossed his face. "Damn, baby, I love you."

"Mmmm," she managed, then pursed her lips for his kiss. As their lips touched, a zing of need rushed down to her clit. His tongue swept past her lips, mating with hers as his hands worked at the knot above their heads.

* * *

A Feast for the Senses

A FEAST FOR THE SENSES

Lisa lay spread out on the kitchen island, her legs dangling from the knee down, the rest of her body supported by the marble surface. Squirming slightly, she readjusted her shoulders and neck without dislodging the layer of plastic wrap that was carefully placed over her naked body and draped around her.

She could hear the buzz of conversations going on all throughout the room, the sudden booms of laughter as someone reacted to a joke, the polite nonsense that everyone was speaking as they milled about the room, mingling with each other. Her lover held several such parties a year, always inviting like minded individuals, those that liked to dabble in power-plays, that got a thrill out of playing D/s games, and those that lived the lifestyle full time.

Last year, she had spent the whole evening clad in a fishnet body suit, her body covered from just under her chin to her wrists, all the way to her ankles, yet flagrantly bare, save for a strip of leather around her waist that draped between her legs, holding the twin dildos trapped inside of her body.

This year, Mark had warned her he had other plans for her than acting as his hostess, but Lisa hadn't imagined he would be so decadent. Her body trembled with repressed need, which was only getting worse as the night continued. On top of the wrap was a layer of food, anything from finger sandwiches to fruits and veggies, and between her legs rested a wooden bowl full of a specially made dip, the long handle of the spoon resting deep inside of her pussy. She could feel the trickle of her cream leaking between her ass-cheeks, probably staining the silk under her.

Mark's guests weren't helping; if anything they seemed to delight in her predicament, subtly thrusting the handle deeper inside of her with each dip of a fruit into the bowl.

One of the guests had even softly stroked fingers over her weeping core, sliding down around the edge to the base of the handle, and back up. The butterfly soft touch only served to inflame her more. Judging by the feel, she would guess it had been a man, but wasn't quite certain.

A fingernail scraped over her right nipple as a guest grabbed a sandwich, the motion repeated harder a second time, then the guest moved off, heels clicking on the hardwood floor. She wanted to scream with frustration, but didn't. Such a sound would only embarrass her lover, so she held it back. Occasionally a soft gasp or moan escaped, but that was all she allowed herself.

The soft leather strips that held her bound to the table, one over her breasts, just above her nipples, one low on her hips, were more decoration that anything. It was her will to please that held her still.

A whisper of his aftershave, the faintest teasing scent alerted her to his presence. Blinded by the silk and mesh scarf over her eyes, she had no way of knowing who was standing beside her, watching the rise and fall of her breasts as she carefully controlled her breathing lest she send the food crashing to the floor, but some sixth sense told her it was Mark -- his warm brown gaze trailing over her body as he admired his handiwork and her submission.

"You're doing so good Lisa, I am so proud of you." Between her legs, the wooden handle was pulled a few inches out, and then thrust back in. Lisa bit her lip to hold back the gasp of pleasure. The motion continued, a soft slid out then a hard thrust, the curved end rubbing against her G-spot until she could feel the material beneath her getting soaked with her essence.

"It's going to be hard to outdo tonight, but I'm sure we can think of something. Don't you luv?"

"Yes," she gasped, unable to control the tremor in her voice. Her pussy was on fire, and the clamp that was wrapped around her clit felt like it was tightening, slowly cutting off all blood flow to the enflamed bundle of nerves. The briefest of flicks against her clit almost sent her into a freefall, but she curled her fingernails into her palms, the flaring of pain giving her control again.

It was becoming harder and harder to hold back, and Lisa was worried that when the party finally ended and Mark claimed her body, that she wouldn't be able to contain her orgasm.

"Mark?"

"Yeah Ed, hang on a second."

"You make me so proud luv. Just a little bit longer, and then I'll have you all to myself." His soft spoken words thrilled her senses. Mark never gave praise lightly; it was always deserved.

Lisa wanted to cry as the handle stilled and the scent of Mark retreated. She focused her breathing, and allowed herself to settle into a haze of sensation, where time drifted by. Sometime later, the scent of Mark's aftershave returned.

"That's the last of them luv. Now it's just you and me, and I have to tell you, I am very, very pleased with you."

Lisa trembled at his praise. Her heart raced as the plastic was lifted off of her, and tossed aside. Slowly, Mark pulled the wooden handle from between her pussylips, and she rocked her hips, prolonging the touch a microsecond more. Her nerves were stretched to their limits by the seemingly unending sensations of the night.

She could feel tears of sexual frustration pooling in her eyes, and blinking furiously, wanting to remove all trace of them before Mark removed her blindfold. She expected him to remove the covering any moment.

Instead, he untied the binding, removing the leather straps from her body. Free to move, she laid there, breathlessly waiting for him to remove her blindfold so she could climb off of the island.

A heated breath whispered across her thigh moments before the soft brush of his hair tickled her skin. Moist lips pressed against her mons, and Lisa moaned softly, knowing that now that they were alone, Mark would want to hear her enjoyment of his touch.

His tongue delved into her already sensitive core, and Lisa screamed softly as she held back the orgasm that slammed against her. Trembling, she whimpered, trying to communicate how close she was to her body betraying her.

"Shhhh luv," Mark whispered against her skin, his breath teasing her even more, "Let yourself go. It's been a long night, and you've done so well."

Free by his leave, she let her muscles loosen and allowed the sensations to swarm over her as he returned to her pussy, his tongue lapping at her heated flesh, spearing deep into her core. She could feel his love with each attentive motion.

Despite his power over her, and her complete submission to him, Mark had never treated her as anything less than an equal. Everything he did was calculated to prolong and increase her pleasure, not to truly torture or demean her.

She submitted, as much as he dominated, out of love.

This time when her orgasm started tremors throughout her body, she let it wash over her. Her pussy tightened, and she could feel the velvet glide of his tongue more intimately as her cream flowed. Back arching at the intensity of the climax, she screamed Mark's name, her hands fisting at her sides. The feel of her fingernails digging into her palms only increased the sensation as Mark reached up her body and pinched her nipples, plucking gently at the tender nubs.

She was softly floating on the euphoria of her orgasm when she felt Mark shift between her legs and heard the unmistakable sound of his belt and zipper being undone. The feel of his dress shirt was replaced by his hips as he slowly and gently pushed his cock into her. Each thrust was carefully drawn out, a slow glide of flesh against flesh. His fingertips danced playfully over his clit as he whispered in her ear, his voice rough with emotion. She couldn't make out the words above the throb of her heart racing, but she knew they were words of love, of praise, of devotion.

Each thrush of Mark's cock pushed her higher, driving her towards another orgasm. When it flowed over her, it was like the warm caress of water lapping at a beach. And it seemed to go on forever, as Mark continued his steady thrusts, wringing every ouch of pleasure out of her body that was possible.

Moaning softly, her body completely worn-out, Lisa barely felt his withdrawal as he slipped from her body and moved around the island to undo her blindfold. Blinking at the muted light, she smiled at his thoughtfulness. Mark had dimmed the lights before coming to her.

She could feel his gaze moving over her. The heat of his possessiveness as he debated what more he wanted from her. She watched as he carefully tucked his erection back into his dress slacks and zipped them up. As tired as she was, Lisa knew she would give him anything he asked for, especially if it meant feeling him release inside of her body, knowing that she brought him to orgasm. It was a heady feeling, being loved by this man.

"Sit up baby."

Groaning softly as the movement, Lisa complied and found her muscles a little stiffer from the forced stillness than she had imagined they would be. Gentle hands cupped her should and started to massage, and Lisa tipped her head back, thankful for his soft touch.

As Mark's hands slid down her back, working tirelessly against her tense muscles, she found her body awakening again. A fire of need started within her breasts and pussy, spreading throughout her body with each swirl of his thumbs over her back, each gentle pinch of his hands.

"Let's get you in the shower," he proclaimed as he reached the curve of her ass. Lisa giggled as his hands touched a ticklish spot. Mark playfully brushed against the spot again before pulling away, and moving to stand in front of her.

With almost careless strength, he picked her up in his arms and carried her into the bedroom, then into the master bath. Setting her down, he reached into the stall and turned on the taps, carefully adjusting the temperature of the three jets before motioning her inside.

Moments later, he had shed his clothing and followed her in. Lisa relaxed against him as he moved to stand behind her, each glide of his body against hers a further enticement. She could feel his need against her back, as his erection brushed against the upper curve of her ass. Her hands itched to reach behind her as cup him, but this was his night.

Sometimes he gave her free reign to touch and tease as she wished, but tonight wasn't one of those times. So she closed her eyes and simply enjoyed the feel of his hands moving over her as she soaped up her body and reaching over them, grabbed the handheld shower jet and washed her off, his movements slow and careful. She knew that there wouldn't be a single drop of soap left on her body when he was through, he was that thorough.

It was one of the things she loved about him, his attention to the slightest detail. It was part of what made him a perfect dominant. Regardless of whether she was tied down and helpless, or held motionless by her own will, she had nothing to fear with him. The lash would never fall on a spot too tender to take another sting, the cuffs would never bind too tight, and her needs would never be neglected for too long.

The shower head nudged against the juncture of her thighs, and she parted them, giving Mark full access. As the warm jets of water pulsed against her clit, she whimpered, her body already craving more.

He didn't make her wait too long. Whether he was tired of teasing, or simply too aroused to draw things out much longer, Mark moved the showerhead back to its holder and turned her in his arms. Lisa's eyes flew open as he cupped her ass and lifted her against him. Instinctively she wrapped her legs around his waist as his cock slid between them, nudging at the opening of her core.

Mark rotated his hips and his cock-head slid past her opening, driving deep within her with his first thrust. Clasping his shoulders, she tipped her head back, trusting him not to let her fall, and enjoyed the feel of his claiming of her body.

A few steps brought her back against the tile covered wall, one of the jets sending a stream of water cascading against her shoulder. Mark's thrusts quickened as he gained leverage. Closing her eyes again, Lisa savored each and every glide of his body against hers, the feel of his chest hairs tickling her nipples, the brush of his groin hair against her clit.

As his mouth claimed her, his tongue sliding past her lips to mate with hers, she embraced the mastery of his touch. Heaven was in his arms, and she was there right then, lost in his touch, in his power over not only her body but over her mind.

She waited with anticipation for his command to come, for his ultimate dominance over her.

As his pace deepened, his cock thrusting harder and faster, her skin sliding against the smooth wet wall, her pussy tightening around his erection, desperate to prolong the sensation, she fell in love with him all over again.

He broke the kiss and dropped his head against her shoulder, his lips brushing against her skin as he let himself go. "That's it baby. Open your body to me, hold me so deep inside you."

Lisa thrilled at his praise as he asserted his claim, his body moments away from marking her with his come. "Oh yeah Lisa, you feel so good baby. So damn good."

Wrapping her arms around his neck, she began rocking against him, drawing out the thrusts of his cock, enhancing the moment for him.

"Damn you feel so good Lisa, so soft and silky and wet. Come for me, tighten your pussy around me to hard then I can never leave you."

The comment in his voice was unmistakable and she couldn't deny him. Clenching his tight, she let her orgasm crest for the second time, her body milking his cock as he spasmed within her, hot jets of come marking her pussy as his, and his alone.

As they struggled to regain their steady breathing, Lisa opened her eyes and shifted to look at Mark's face. His eyes closed, long lashed laying against his cheeks, he looked like an angel to her.

She knew some would judge her for her complete submission to her, say she was betraying her gender and all women had struggled to attain, but they had no clue. In submitting to Mark she freed herself, and she lived her life as she chose.

As his eyes opened and she met the beautiful blue of his gaze, she pressed a soft kiss against his lips. "I love you," she whispered against his firm lips and felt whispered back to her.

The chill of the water forced an end to the moment, but as Mark carried her out of the shower and carefully set her down, and dried her off, she knew that another memory would soon be in the making.

Judging by his returning erection, he wasn't done with her yet.

KINKY GIRLS DO

* * *

CHASING HER DREAM

Lydia pulled the top off her third pint of Ben & Jerry's, and dug her spoon in. Licking the delicious chocolate chip cookie dough ice cream from the underside of the spoon, she slid it into her mouth and moaned softly. Although she wasn't feeling much better, the sugar rush was helping some. She hated feeling depressed on her birthday. Depressed, and dumped only made it that much worse.

A hard pounding on her front door drew her attention away from her comfort food. She sat there and listened to the sound of a fist hitting wood, completely unwilling to get up and see who it was.

"Lydia, open the door, dammit!"

Oh great, just what I need. Good guy Shawn coming to my rescue. Shawn, who I have been lusting over since before I started dating Smucko, she thought to herself, before hollering "Go away!"

"Not until I make sure that you're all right."

Grimacing, she set down her ice cream and headed to the door. She paused along the way to pull her robe on over her pajamas. Unlocking it, she swung it open and confronted her unwanted visitor. "I'm alive. You happy now?"

"Nope." Typical of his take charge behavior, Shawn shouldered past her into the living room. Lydia watched in shock as he plopped down onto her sofa and picked up her ice cream. "Cookie dough. My favorite."

It was him dipping her spoon into her ice cream that drew Lydia out of her stupor. "That's mine!" she snarled as she yanked it from his hands. Shawn let the ice cream go, only to clasp her hips in his large hands and pull her into his lap.

"There, now that I've got your attention, tell me what happened."

Lydia struggled to get up, but weakened by a day of crying and heartache, she soon gave up and settled into the warmth and comfort her friend offered. "He broke up with me."

"I know that part. He told me at the gym. When he told me that he left you crying, and laughed about it, I hit him."

"He laughed about it?" If anything, it made her feel worse. Struggling to hold back the fresh tears, she scooped another spoonful of ice cream up and licked it off the spoon.

"Sorry, I shouldn't have told you that." Shawn pulled the ice cream from her hands and set it aside before he continued. "It made him feel like a big man or something. Although all of the guys were fairly pissed at him, and I know if I hadn't, several of them would have hit him themselves."

"I'm glad you hit him," she mumbled against his chest as she burrowed into his warmth. Although her relationship has just ended, it wasn't the fact that it was over that hurt; it was how much she had misjudged her ex. She knew she would get over him, but wasn't sure how long it would take her to trust a new guy.

"So, what happened?"

Shawn's warm hand clasped the back of her neck, tipping her head to the side, and then he ran his fingers through her hair. She wanted to melt into him, it felt so good.

"We had a fight. He called me a sexual deviant and he wanted nothing to do with me."

"You? A sexual deviant?" Lydia could feel the rumble of his laughter deep in his chest. "You're too sweet to be a deviant, sexual or otherwise."

Hysterical laughter bubbling within her, Lydia retorted, "I thought so too. But evidently I am."

"Just what is it you wanted to try?"

Her cheeks hot, Lydia burrowed further against his chest, inhaling deeply of Shawn's cologne. Just his scent was enough to get her hot, it always had. "I don't want to talk about it."

His hand left her hair and moved to her chin, cupping it and forcing her head up. Lydia struggled to meet his gaze, even as she wished he would just let the whole thing drop.

"Since when have we had secrets from each other?" If only he knew just what all I am keeping secret, she thought.

"It's too embarrassing." Lydia imagined Shawn's gaze peering into her soul as he continued to just look at her.

Pulling away from his hand, she dipped her chin to her chest and sat up, bending her legs and wrapping her arms around them. "Since it's my birthday he asked if I had anything I wanted to try. And I told him that I wanted him to dominate me."

"Pardon?" Shawn asked, his voice cracking.

Lydia smiled sadly. "I didn't want him to hurt me, or anything like that. I just wanted him to dominant me. Tie me up, spank me, and maybe some light role-play. I just wanted to feel helpless, completely at his mercy. And he did ask..."

Despite clearing his throat, Shawn's voice was still raspy when he spoke. "And was it just him you envisioned doing this? Or is it a fantasy of yours and you were willing to let him play the part?"

"Just let him, I guess. He's not exactly the overpowering type. But I was willing to settle for him, if he'd at least consider it."

"And let me guess, when you told him, he freaked, right?"

Lydia nodded, completely miserable. Now that he had forced the answer out of her, Shawn probably thought she was a freak, too.

As his hand cupped her chin, she tried to resist, but he gently prevailed, forcing her gaze up to meet his. "He wasn't the right man for you, Lydia. He's not man enough for you. You intimidated him."

She couldn't believe it, instead of pushing her away; he was trying to make her feel better. Maybe he didn't think she was such a freak.

"Look at you, a successful entrepreneur with your own advertising company, and you're just twenty-five. The only thing he ever started on his own was a lemonade stand in elementary school. And that failed miserably."

A giggle escaped before she could control it. In answer, Shawn's lips curved into a grin. "It's true. We got drunk one night and he told me all about it. Showed me pictures his mom took, too. And that's another problem, he's a momma's boy. He probably needed you to dominate him, not hand the reins over to him."

Remembering all the times that she had had to take control, she nodded.

"Well, there you have it. What you need is a man who is secure enough in his masculinity to be willing to let you dominate, and to fulfill your fantasies, including letting you submit to him. And I know the perfect guy for you."

"You do?" Afraid of which one of his friends he was going to try to set her up with, she almost didn't ask. She didn't want one of his friends. She wanted him.

"Yeah, I do." Without any warning, his head swooped down and his lips pressed against hers. Unconsciously, her lips parted beneath his, allowing his tongue entrance into her mouth. All too quickly, it was over. "Me."

Lydia giggled again, hoping she hadn't heard him wrong; her ears were still ringing from that kiss. But afraid to act in case she had.

"Let me prove it to you."

Still shocked, she just nodded.

"Run."

"Wha-at?"

"Get up off of my lap, and run. And when I catch you, I expect you to put up a fight."

On shaky legs, Lydia stood and moved around the couch. Like a deer caught in headlights, she remained there, waiting for him to move. His head whipped around, his gaze locking on her. She wasn't certain what she saw in his eyes, but it had never been there before. He looked almost—feral.

"I. Said. Run," he bit out and stood.

With a shriek, Lydia took off, running out of the living room, her bathrobe flaring around her hips. She turned the corner and paused, peeking back into the living room in time to see him leap off the couch and move across the room like a panther, stalking his prey.

Her bare feet slapped against the hardwood stairs as she hurried up, Shawn hot on her heels. As she reached the top, she could hear his breath right behind her. He reached out a hand, and she barely darted away, pushing into her office and slamming the door.

Shawn pounded on the door, then tried the knob. As the door swung open, he was wearing a triumphant grin. Lydia backed away from him as he crossed the room towards her. This wasn't the Shawn she knew, the calm and controlled gentleman.

Just as he was about to grab her, she ducked under his outstretched arm and raced away. Panting with her exertions and the thrill of being chased, she raced back down the stairs. Shawn pounded down behind her, and succeeded in tackling her at the base of the stairs. Even as she fell, she registered him turning to cushion her fall with his body.

Trapped against his chest, she wiggled, trying to get away. His strong hands clasped her around the waist, his legs locked around hers, holding her pinned. She wiggled, thrilled at the sensation of his hard cock digging into her back. Suddenly, she didn't have the will to struggle anymore. She was aroused, and she had a feeling that he was more than aware of it. If she had to bet on it, she would lay her money on her panties being soaked by now.

"You done struggling now?" Shawn whispered in her ear, his breath tickling the sensitive lobe. In response, she renewed her struggles, but soon gave up. She was well and truly pinned.

"Good girl. Now I'm going to let you go and you're going to walk slowly and sweetly up the stairs. If I have to chase you again, it won't go well for you." There was the briefest hint of steel to his voice, which only served to cause Lydia's pulse to flutter. She wanted to protest that she had only made him chase her because he told her to, but this was what she had been dreaming of—Shawn bending her to his will. She couldn't have planned a better birthday if she had tried.

Nodding her head against his chest, she agreed to behave herself.

His arms and legs relaxed, allowing her to climb off him. As she stepped away, he rocked up onto his shoulders, pulled his feet up, and kicked out, thrusting himself upright. The fluidity of his movements, the sheer power had her jaw dropping. She had seen him do some interesting moves like that when they had worked out together and he had taught her to defend herself, which coincidentally was where she discovered how much she liked being pinned down—by the right man.

But she didn't have time to drool as she would have liked because he moved towards her, herding her backwards. That look was back in his eyes, the one that screamed dominant male.

As she turned and headed back up the stairs, she could feel him looming behind her, the heat of his skin radiating against her. She shivered at the images it evoked: his nude sweat-drenched body covering her as he held her wrists pinned in one hand, the other holding him up as he thrust into her.

When she reached the landing, she paused. Shawn leaned in, his breath hot and moist against her neck. "Having second thoughts?"

Lydia shook her head and forced a simple "no," past her parched lips. Licking them, she tried to vocalize her dilemma. "Do you want me to change? Or just, um, strip."

"I want you to go into the bedroom, and then I'm going to do what I want to you, when I want. You'll wait, wondering what I want you to do next. What I will do to you next."

If Shawn's hand hadn't pressed gently against her back, Lydia wasn't sure she would have been able to move, the idea was so delicious. Helpless, completely bending to his will, his whims.

Shawn stopped her as she reached the bed and turned her around, pulling her into his arms. "I wanted to go slow," he growled, "to savor you this first time. But I've waited so long."

His mouth crashed down over hers, his tongue taking possession of her mouth. Lydia almost fainted at the sweet euphoria flooding through her. This was what she had always wanted, not the lukewarm passion she had settled for. As she submitted completely to his touch, she felt freer than she ever dreamed she could.

Shawn cupped her ass, gently kneading the flesh as he pulled her tighter into his body. His legs bracketed hers, holding her tucked against the cradle of his body. He tore his lips from her.

"How I want you," he whispered, his voice trembling with emotions Lydia couldn't even begin to separate and define.

Stepping back, he twisted them around so that his back was to the bed. Slowly, he sat down, his hands retaining a firm grip on her hips. "Now, strip for me."

Shyly Lydia stepped back and raised her hands to her hair, pulling the tresses free from the clip holding them up. As the silken strands settled about her shoulders, she turned her back to him. Untying the belt of her robe, she quickly let it slid to the floor. Unbuttoning her pajama top, she let it dip slightly back, baring the briefest hint of shoulders, before letting it slip completely to the floor, her breasts bared to the air-conditioned air circulating throughout the room.

She paused, uncertain. She could hear Shawn breathing harshly behind her, but even as she knew he wanted her, she wasn't certain just what to do. Having a fantasy was one thing—knowing how to carry it out, completely different.

"Turn around."

Lydia obeyed the command in his voice, her chin tucked against her chest. She could hear the bed creak as he stood. His fingers were firm and gentle as Shawn cupped her chin, forcing her gaze to his.

"Continue."

After loosening the tie of her pajama bottoms, she gave them a soft push, sliding them down her legs, to pool at her feet. All that was left was her panties, and she would be bared to Shawn's knowing eyes. Her gaze still locked on his, she grabbed the ties at the sides of her thong and tugged, sending it floating to the floor.

As his eyes drifted over her, she trembled, knowing what he was seeing; the hard beads of her nipples begging to be touched, the faint tan lines of her bathing suit, her smooth shaven pussy, and her lips glistening with the beginnings of her desire. And all she could do was stand there, while he was scanning her, taking her in.

Unable to stand the suspense, she closed her eyes. If anything it made it worse. Now she was lost, wondering where he was looking, unable to see his eyes and know what he was thinking.

It was definitely the best, but most emotionally draining and oddly exhilarating birthday she had ever had. And from what Shawn had said, it was only the beginning.

Lydia jumped as his knuckles brushed against her neck, trailing down her shoulder to the upper curve of her breast. "He was a fool."

Opening her eyes, she smiled at how dark and deep his eyes appeared. His hand continued its path, trailing down her ribs to her waist, where it stopped. He applied the slightest pressure as he stepped back, drawing her to the bed, where he once more sat down.

"Come here," he said, patting his thighs. When she moved to straddle him, he shook his head. "No, lay across them."

He couldn't be asking what she thought. As she awkwardly lay down across his thighs he made no move to stop her, and she knew he did mean it. He was actually going to spank her.

But he didn't. Instead, his hand gently traced up and down her back and over the smooth curves of her ass. Lydia relaxed against him, soothed by his touch, even as in the back of her mind a voice screamed that she was bare-ass naked over a fully-clothed man's lap—her best friend's lap at that.

Shawn's fingers started to dip and tease, no longer as soothing, as he gently thrust into her core, massaging the tiny bud of her clit with his thumb.

Lydia twitched on his lap, her hands braced against the floor. She could feel the slick inner walls of her pussy clenching around his fingers, begging him silently for more.

"Like this?" He asked, his voice husky with need.

She moaned softly in answer.

"Good. How about this?" And that was all the warning she received before his palm landed with a solid smack!

She jerked, emitting a faint yelp. Fingers of fire spread through her ass, trailing directly to her clit. "Do you want more?"

"Yes," she panted, closing her eyes in anticipation. Shawn thrust his fingers deep, and then landed another blow.

Lydia jerked under the sweet sting, raising her ass slightly for more, which he gave three smacks in quick succession. Followed by his fingers doing things inside of her she couldn't describe but caused her toes to curl.

"How old is the birthday girl today, twenty-five? Should she get a swat for each year?"

Her ass was already on fire, and he wanted to do twenty more? Oh, God, she would die first. But what a way to go.

"Yes, please, Shawn." And he granted her wish, drawing each swat out as he played her body like a fine tuned instrument, tugging just hard enough on her clit to produce the most exquisite sensation, before doubling it with another hard spank.

She was sure she wouldn't be able to sit for a week, but she didn't care. His hot breath sounded harsh between the swats, a perfect match for her own panting gasps as she twisted on his lap, eager for more at the same time she questioned if she could take it.

"Please, Shawn," she panted. Her pussy was on fire, her ass stung, and she wanted nothing more than to feel him driving into her, his hard cock claiming her in a millennium's old ritual of male domination.

"Just one more, baby," he answered, "you can take it."

As his palm landed the final blow, he thrust a third finger into her core. Lydia screamed as sensations erupted through her body, pleasure blending with pain until she didn't know where one began and the other ended. She floated in the euphoria, completely pliant to his hands as he moved her from his lap to the bed.

She opened her eyes to find Shawn standing between her legs, his hands fisted at his side. His nostrils flared with each breath he took. Tormented need twisted his lips into a frown, and his eyes were closed.

"Shawn?" She hesitantly sat up, her hands reaching out to him. "Did I do something wrong?"

"God, no!" he exploded as his eyes flew open. "I just want...but I don't want to hurt you."

"Hurt me?"

"I want to fuck you." Lydia gasped at his crudeness. This wasn't the Shawn she was used to seeing, but it was the one she had always hoped for. "I've been dreaming about it for weeks, fantasizing about laying you over my lap and spanking your rounded ass until you come, then slamming into you so hard your teeth rattle. But if I do, I'm going to hurt you, and you'll never let me be with you again."

"Shawn, you won't hurt me." But he didn't seem to be listening; lost in his own fears. Just as she had been when the fantasies of being dominated had started.

Relaxing back into the bed, she bent her knees and lifted her feet, pressing her heels against the curve of the mattress. Parting her legs as wide as they would go, she opened herself, even as she trembled. She felt completely exposed. Fisting her hands in the sheets, she waited. Her gaze locked with Shawn's, she could see his struggle. Although her mind rebelled at what she was doing, her heart demanded she say it. "Master, please."

Shawn's eyes widened and he seemed to actually see her for the first time since she laid back.

"I need you."

Shawn's hands slid up her thighs, trembling as he caressed her. Lydia responded by widening the cradle of her thighs, offering herself to him. It was the ultimate submission, beyond any fantasy she had ever had, and she was willing to make it for Shawn. But only for him.

He widened his stance, his gaze meeting hers. "Are you sure?"

"As you wish, Shawn. I'm yours."

His hands dropped to his waist, and pulled his shirt free, tossing it over his shoulder. He unbuttoned his jeans and pulled then down his hips, but left them on. He gave a tug to the opening of his boxers, pulling the button completely off. Lydia trembled as his cock sprang free, as thick and hard as she had imagined it to be when she was laying over his lap.

"Put your arms over your head." The steel was back in this voice. She watched in silence as he reached into her nightstand and pulled out an unopened box on condom. Tearing the foil with his teeth, he slowly rolled the latex over his erection. Lydia's mouth watered at the sight; she wanted to curl her tongue around his cock-head and suck on the reddened flesh until he grabbed her hair and held her still, so he could thrust deep into her mouth. Her pussy clenched at the knowledge that maybe later he would. But first, she wanted to feel him deep in her core, claiming her body as his.

With one hand on his cock, Shawn lifted his other to hers, encircling her wrists, pinning them against the mattress as he restrained her, the fine matting of hair on his chest tickling her nipples.

Once more, his fingers did things to her, things she had never imagined as they manipulated her clit and lips. She bucked against him, desperate for deeper contact, as he teased her with his cock head, brushing it against her pussy-lips.

Just when she was about to cry out in frustration, he thrust hard, driving his cock deep within her. Lydia screamed at the sudden invasion, even as she wrapped her legs around his waist to hold him there. His hand moved from their joining, bracing on the bed.

She arched her back, pressing her breasts against his chest as he started to thrust, pounding into her willing flesh. His teeth bit into her neck, marking her as his, and she loved it.

Shawn's sweat mingled with hers, coating them both, as he claimed her, driving them both closer to the edge.

Lydia's pussy ached, clenching him tight as he withdrew, then tighter as she thrust back. She lost track of time, as she was enveloped in sensation. This was her fantasy, and then some.

And then she thought no more, as with a savage thrust, Shawn pushed her into orgasm. Hoarse screams filled the room, and she dimly recognized them as her own, but couldn't, and wouldn't make them stop.

It was only as his voice joined hers, shouting out his release before he collapsed on top of her, that she stopped. His hold on her wrists slackened, and she wrapped her arms around his neck, holding him pressed against her.

"Happy birthday, baby," Shawn whispered.

"Mmm," she murmured back, too sated to bother with words. And despite the awful beginning to the day, it was looking to be the best birthday yet.

* * *

COWBOY'S DUNGEON

Moving with a smooth grace, Natalie hung her Stetson on the hat-hook just inside the barn door, and then stepped into her husband's playroom. Over the years, he had slowly added more and more sex toys, until the room could rival any dungeon of depravity. She paused just inside the threshold and inhaled deeply, savoring the scent of tanned leather, sweat, and sex. If she listened closely, she could almost hear the echoes of her moans and screams from the night before.

Trembling as the memory fanned the embers of her lingering passion, Natalie continued her journey into the room. Ahead of her, along the back wall, stood a giant wooden cross where her husband often strapped her by her wrists and ankles, and whipped her ass to a rosy hue. Whips, paddles, and chains adorned one wall, while along the other a row of mirrors gave an air of class to the rustic room.

As she reached the center of the room, Natalie paused again. She ran her fingers over the waist high, saddled "horse," and felt the crotch of her jeans growing damp.

Attached to the ceiling, the homemade horse was a curious contraption; it was made up of a wooden bench with a saddle laid over it. It was held in place by ropes run through a series of pulleys and levers, and hung a few feet from the floor. At the flick of a switch, a motor started that would cause Andrew's invention to rock, tipping slightly forward and back with each motion. The saddle was a traditional western saddle; the stirrups adjusted to the perfect length to help Natalie remain balanced as she rode.

A quick glance at her watch elicited a gasp from Natalie's lips. It was almost three p.m., and Andrew had ordered her to be mounted and ready for him right on the hour. Hurriedly, Natalie moved to the row of mirrors and stripped. She neatly folded her clothes, laying them on a bench in the corner.

Crossing the room, she pulled a leather harness and a vibrator from one of the shelves, as well as a large tube of lubricant. She coated the dildo with the clear gel before she slid it into her pussy an inch at a time. By the time the toy was in to the hilt, beads of sweat formed on her brow. She wanted to lie down on the floor and fuck herself to an orgasm, but Andrew would somehow know, and she wasn't about to do anything to upset her master.

After a quick wiggle of her hips to make sure the dildo was firmly in place, Natalie stepped into the harness, and pulled it up her waist, setting the strap between her thighs to hold the toy in place. She made quick work of the many buckles and straps, familiarity making her task easy.

Once she had the fake cock secured deep inside her body, Natalie stepped back up to the suspended horse and mounted. With moments to spare, Natalie had time to reflect on the toy that was buried within her clenching pussy.

Firm, and curved at the tip, it was her favorite dildo. With every breath, the head pressed and rubbed against her sensitive walls. She couldn't help but moan softly and shift, manipulating the cock to press against her g-spot.

Minutes passed, as the leather saddle beneath her ass grew slick from her sweat and her essence. Gripping the pommel, Natalie squirmed and wiggled; trying to find relief, which she knew wasn't available to her. The dildo nestled deep within her was designed to make her aware of every nerve-ending in her pussy. It was intended to increase her sexual frustration, to heighten her pleasure - and Andrew's. Only with the swinging motions of the horse would she achieve orgasm.

Gazing at herself in the wall of mirrors was another form of sensual torture that Andrew demanded. She could see her nipples standing out hard and proud from her chest, tiny silver rings dangling from the tips. Her skin glistened with a fine sheen of sweat. The ropes holding the horse in place creaked as Natalie shifted again.

A faint breeze stirred the air as Andrew opened the barn door, announcing his presence.

"Been waiting long?" he drawled.

"No Sir. I was mounted and ready at three." Keeping her gaze focused on her reflection in the mirror, Natalie fought the urge to squirm again.

The long curved vibrator pressed directly on her g-spot, and she craved to succumb to the gushing orgasm it could bring.

She could hear Andrew's steps behind her as he crossed the room and settled into his chair. Natalie knew it wouldn't be long now. She heard the flick of the switch in the stillness of the room, and had a moment to draw a deep breath before the motor started manipulating the ropes in the pulleys.

As the horse bucked back and forth, grinding the pommel against the base of the harness, Natalie gripped the saddle horn tight. Digging the arches of her feet firmly in the stirrups, she tightened her thigh muscles and held on for the ride.

The smooth leather beneath her ass rubbed her inner thighs and butt-cheeks as she shifted backward. On the back swing, she shifted forward.

Faster and faster the horse rocked, until Natalie couldn't control her reactions any more. Moaning and arching against the pommel, she drove the cock as far into her quivering pussy as the harness allowed and climaxed deliciously. She loved climaxing this way, the rocking motions of invention almost a mirror for the gate of a real horse. The only difference was, with a flick of a switch, Andrew could vary the speed, and withhold her orgasm for hours if he chose. The fact that he had allowed her to come so quickly meant he had other plans in mind. She shivered in delicious curiosity as to what those plans were, but knew better than to ask.

The motions of Andrew's invention slowed, until it only swayed slightly.

"Did you like that?"

"Yes, Sir," Natalie whispered, her breath coming in gasps. What she really wanted was another ride, this time with him joining her, and his cock buried in her pussy.

"Dismount." The slow drawl of his voice was gone, replaced by clipped forcefulness. Andrew was a country boy at heart, but he was also a very dominant man.

Legs shaking, Natalie slid from the horse and stood waiting. Bracing herself with a hand on the damp leather, she turned to face her husband. His damp, curly hair, clean jeans and flannel shirt made it obvious he had stopped for a shower after tending to the fence in the east pasture. He had pulled on his clean boots, which lacked the mud and manure that clung to his work boots.

"Come over here, and bring a paddle with you."

Mind racing, Natalie tried to think of what she had done to deserve punishment. Walking across the room as fast as her legs would carry her, Natalie quickly selected his favorite paddle and presented herself to Andrew. Dropping to her knees, she laid her head on his inner thigh and waited, the paddle clutched in her hands.

He smelled of sandalwood soap and leather, of sex and cologne.

Inhaling deeply, Natalie resisted her desire to nuzzle her nose in his crotch. She loved to bury her face in the tiny curls of hair around the base of his cock after he had showered.

"Climb up here," he demanded, patting his thighs. Her legs less shaky, Natalie stood at Andrew's side. After handing him the paddle, she bent over at the waist, and let him guide her into position over his thighs.

"I want you to know something, Natalie. I love you, but you deserve a paddling. You left the door open on the chicken pen, and we lost several good hens. So be a good girl, take your punishment, and we can move on to the real reason we're out here."

The paddle smacked against her damp flesh.

Yelping softly, she relaxed her body, eager for the next swat. Again the paddle smacked her tingling flesh.

She knew she had made a mistake and deserved punishment. While she enjoyed the paddle's sting, she knew that every time she sat down over the next day would be a reminder for her to double check the pens.

Another smack came, this one harder than the last. Natalie winced slightly at the sting, even as her pussy clenched around the dildo.

Again and again Andrew rained blows on her tender ass, until they melted into in a continuous blur of euphoric sensations. Each instinctive jerk of her body twitched the harness, shifting the cock that was still strapped within her.

Lost in the slow build of her second orgasm, Natalie at first didn't notice the paddle had stopped falling.

"I think that's enough for now. You should be nice and tender for a while."

Natalie wanted to wail 'no', to demand that he swat her a few more times.

Her pussy was already gripping spasmodically around the dildo. Just a few more swats would send her over the edge.

She knew better than to beg for more. This was Andrew's domain, and in here, she did as she was told. She also knew any more swats might make a gentle reminder a painful one, so he truly had stopped for her.

"Stand up."

Legs weak, Natalie complied. Andrew smoothly stood, his toned body rippling with the motion. His flannel shirt pulled tight against his corded muscles. Natalie felt her legs waver as always, watching his movements.

"Remove your harness darlin', and bend over and grab the arms of the chair."

The smooth drawl she loved so much was back, melting her a little more inside. When she had first met Andrew, his voice was so smooth that she had nearly creamed her pants with their first conversation. Nothing had changed in the five years since.

With shaking hands, she worked to remove the harness. She was always surprised that it took longer to strip off the harness than it took to buckle it into place. As the dildo slid free from her weeping pussy lips, Natalie shuddered and almost collapsed into a puddle on the hardwood floor. Her clit throbbed, aching for contact.

Resisting the urge to finger herself to another orgasm, Natalie bent over and gripped the arms of Andrew's chair so tightly her knuckles turned white.

"Relax." Andrew stroked a finger gently up and down her spine. His callused hands moved over her tense muscles and relaxed her.

Slipping his fingers down to her ass-cheeks, he gently parted the globes and slid a fingertip into her crack. He teased around her sensitive nether hole, making her scream silently in her mind for the penetration. As if he heard her thoughts, he pressed a finger on her hungry orifice, past the gripping muscles. Pushing firmly, he worked his finger and slid it all the way in, stretching her tight rosebud.

"Relax," he drawled again.

Natalie's head fell forward and she turned slightly so she could see almost everything Andrew was doing in the mirrors. She felt empty as he removed his finger from her anus. She watched in the mirror as he bent forward and picked up the tube of lubricant from the floor.

Popping the top, he pressed the tip against her puckered hole and squeezed.

The cool liquid trickled into her hole and coated her crack. Recapping the tube, he tossed it aside and reached behind his back and pulled something from the back pocket of his pants. Natalie almost whimpered as she saw the size of the butt-plug in his hand. Natalie found it odd looking, with the tuft of long horsehair attached to the base.

Pressing it firmly against her ass-bud, Andrew twisted the plug as her muscles stretched and then gave way, the flared base lodging tightly against her anus.

"On your hands and knees," he ordered.

Natalie tried to gracefully drop to the ground, but the sensation of the large plug nestled in her ass caused her to twitch and shudder along the way. As she settled herself, she felt the tail brush against the back of her thighs. "Tell me what you're feeling baby. Let me know how much you love being touched, my hands stroking along your flank."

At first she opened her mouth to respond, but as he stroked his hands over her back and along her thighs, she realized just what Andrew was asking for. He'd been having her read pony-play erotica on the internet, and from all of their role-playing before, she had pleased him the most when she stayed true to character. Trying to mimic the sounds of their horses, she tossed her head back and neighed.

"Good girl." Andrew's praise encouraged her work harder to imitate what she had never before tried. Shifting her hips, Natalie tried to prance slightly, without being told. Around his chair she circled, showing off her sleek lines.

After her fourth turn, Andrew reached out a restraining hand. Gripping her hair tightly, he pulled her head back. "Shhhh girl. It's ok baby. Stand still."

Natalie trembled as his hands stroked down her spine, along her side and around to the mound of her mons.

"You're such a nice filly. Someone has been taking very good care of you, haven't they?"

Andrew stood and moved around behind her. He held her still with just a finger thrust into her creamy heat. Natalie could hear the sound of his zipper being undone behind her. Pretending nervousness, she shifted from side to side, whinnying softly and nodding her head back.

"Shhh girl. Shhhh. No one's going to hurt you. Just relax. That's a good girl." Andrew kept up a steady stream of soft-spoken words as he moved her tail to the side, pressed his cock against her pussy lips, and thrust.

"Oh yeah, such a good filly."

Natalie clenched her pussy tight as Andrew withdrew and thrust in again, deeply. His hands gripped her hips, holding her still for his assault.

She wanted to beg him, to go harder, to fuck her senseless, but she also didn't want to lose her role in their game.

Neighing louder, she hoped to convey her demands. Tossing her hair, she arched her back and gripped his cock tighter.

One of Andrew's hands left her hips and tangled in her hair, pulling her head back farther. "You like that, little filly?"

Natalie neighed as she pushed back into the curve of his groin.

"You like being ridden rough?" His fingers dug tighter into her hip as he pulled her head back. Leaning down, Andrew bit the side of her neck as he slammed into her pussy, covering her as a stallion would a mare. He savaged her willing flesh, taking her with an unexplored animalistic passion.

Natalie knew she would sport some bruises in the morning, but didn't care.

Her body screamed for more, lost within a maelstrom of passion. Her voice hoarse from neighing so much, she whispered Andrew's name softly, her body convulsing in orgasm.

Quivering, she felt Andrew pounding into her pussy, until with one last thrust he collapsed against her back, pushing them both to the hardwood floor.

Natalie struggled to regain her breath as her body hummed. Feeling completely drained and lethargic, she couldn't summon the energy to roll over when Andrew flopped to his side next to her.

His hand stroked down her back to her ass, where he grabbed the base and gently removed the plug.

"I love you, baby," he drawled, his voice husky. Tenderly, he placed soft kisses along her back and still rosy ass-cheeks.

"I love you too, Master."

"As much as I would love to lay here all night kissing and caressing you, I think we are in need of a shower." Andrew stood and helped Natalie up, then swept her into his arms.

"Thank you," she whispered. She nestled her head in the crook of his neck as he carried her out the barn door. "I love you too, Andrew."

"My pleasure darlin'. You did well, very well. There are some more things I want to try out, real soon."

* * *

MICHELLE HOUSTON

ALL ABOUT TRUST

As time passed, Melissa found her mind wandering. Gregory had blindfolded her earlier, and asked her to wait on him. She wasn't about to move and risk upsetting him. Which was how she found herself laying on her bed, her hands tied together and positioned over her heads, with nothing to do but think. Just like her lover had planned.

Gregory had proposed the night before, and as much as she loved him, as much as she cherished him in her life, she wasn't certain if she could take that last step – and trust him with their future. It was one thing to trust him with her body, but the knowledge of how quickly relationships could sour made her hesitate. She knew that hurt him, but he had taken it in stride.

At least she had thought so, until he had bound her hands, blindfolded her, and asked her to think about their relationship, and where she saw them going – if anywhere.

Unable to think about her future without considering how she had gotten to the present, she found herself reflecting on how things started in high school. She had been lucky with her pick of men; they had all been relatively good guys. But therein lay part of the problem-- they were all too good.

Yet, as much as she had dreamed of a certain type of bad boy, she hadn't dared risk the heartache that such a man could bring. She had seen it too frequently in her mom's own failed relationships. Time after time, she had opened herself up, and suffered for it. Some of the men had simply been unable to commit; others were users and abusers.

College hadn't been much better for Melissa. There was Aaron, whose idea of kinky had been to watch her strip for him, Scott who couldn't handle the idea of tying her up, let alone dominating her, and Patrick, sweet adorable Patrick, who had a submissive streak of his own. All nice, good guys. The kind of man she should have leaped on after the experiences of her childhood, but something had always been missing, and she knew it.

Three years out in the 'real world' after college hadn't yielded much better results. Until a chance meeting, thanks to a mutual friend, had introduced her to Gregory. The man she loved. The man who she wasn't certain she could marry.

Jerked from her memories at the sound of the bedroom door opening, Melissa started trembling. Time was up.

She felt the bed dip as Gregory joined her, the subtle scent of his cologne deliciously mixing with the night air.

"Did you miss me?" His hands slid slowly up her hip. Melissa trembled at the touch, her body instantly primed and ready to go off, despite the turmoil of her thoughts. She knew it would be a while before he would be ready to let her.

"Yes," she whispered, licking her dry lips.

Gregory leaned down and kissed her, his tongue gliding along the seam of her lips, further moistening them. Shifting restlessly, she parted her legs further, as her clit throbbed. The clamp around it caused a rush of moisture to pool under her hips.

Gregory's smooth hands cupped her breasts, fingers pinching her nipples as she lay passive beneath him, knowing to arch into his touch would displease him, and after the hurt of last night, she didn't want to do anything else that would upset him. Even if it was something so simple as moving without his permission.

He had only asked her to lay still and to think, it really wasn't so much.

"Are you all wet for me Melissa?"

"Yes."

"You're not lying to me, are you?"

"No Gregory," she responded, aching for him to doubt her. As she felt the warm, dry touch of his fingertip trailing around her stomach, she held her breath. It could go either way--either he would allow her the small glide of his fingers inside her pussy, which experience had taught her would only ignite her need, or he would take her word for it and tease and torment her in others ways.

Either way, it was going to be a while before he let her orgasm.

"You're sure you're not lying to me?" His fingertip brushed along the tiny auburn patch of hair he allowed her to keep on her mound. Her lips had to be smoothly shaven each morning, ready for his oral attention at any time. She didn't want to ever risk giving him whisker burn. Gregory had shown the same care each time he took her to bed, making sure to rid himself of his thick whiskers any time even a hint of them started to show.

But that one patch of hair, so long as it was kept neatly trimmed at no longer than an inch, she kept. And Gregory let her, knowing she liked to trail her fingers through it before she manipulated the tiny bud of her clit.

He liked it too, using it as a favored caressing spot as he teased her having discovered just how sensitive the skin beneath it was.

"I swear Gregory, I'm not lying." She had before though, when he told her to. It had earned her an ass-spanking that fired her senses just thinking about it. But this time he hadn't made that demand.

He heaved a wearied sign, and she could picture she sparkle in his brown eyes as he slid his finger down further, flicking it over her engorged clit, before slipping between her lips. Pumping the one digit into her core, he stroked the slick inner walls of her pussy, increasing her need a notch before pulling back.

"You were telling the truth baby, and I'm sorry for doubting you. Let me make it up to you?"

"If you wish," she gasped out, already knowing just how he would make it up to her. Melissa focused on keeping her muscles relaxed as he climbed off of the bed and circled to the other side. Gently grasping her wrists, he pulled some of the slack in the sash that bound her wrists together, and tied it around her headboard. Her leg trembled as he moved down the bed and cupped her slender ankle. Lifting it to his lips, he sucked one toes into his mouth, one at a time, lavishing them with attention. Her clit throbbed in protest, demanding he shift his attention there. But he didn't.

Instead, he carefully tied her ankle to another scarf, this one previously having been attached to the footboard. Her other foot received the same tongue attention, before being bound, and then he was at her head.

Melissa could hear the faint sounds of her nightstand drawer being opened, and her mind raced, wondering which toy her was going to pull out. Last time he had used the anal plug, so she doubted he would use it again so soon, but there were dozens of other alternatives.

She jerked as his hand suddenly cupped her breasts, thumb and forefinger pulling her nipple into a hard bud. The familiar sting of a gator clamp soon followed. As he repeated the process on the other breast, he moved slower, leaning over her body to brush her stinging nipple with the smooth silk of his shirt.

Melissa whimpered in pained-pleasure.

"Do you like my apology so far baby?"

"Yes," she hissed out, her nipples on fire.

"Good." He fairly purred, and Melissa creamed at the sound. He had a sadistic streak that he rarely indulged, but some times, he was all too willing to torment her to her limits. Given his mood when he had left her, she well understood that he wouldn't let her off easy this time.

Spread eagle and fully bound, she should have felt dirty with her nipple and clit clamps, but only felt free. It wasn't until she had met Gregory, and he had first spanked her, that she had felt herself truly come alive. Gregory pushed her, and she allowed him to, even begging him to upon occasion.

All her past relationships had been pale shadows of what she now enjoyed.

Even with the fears of the past, she had been able to see that he was the best thing that had ever happened to her. Yet, she could remember her mother expressing the same sentiments about husband number three.

The faint whistle in the air was the only warning she got before the nine-tailed whip landed against her skin. Hissing at the sting on her stomach, she wanted badly to see her skin turning from creamy white to red.

Another faint switch, then the whip connected with her left breast. She undulated on the bed, her pussy clenching, aching for a hard cock to fill her, as he lashed at her again, this time marking her right breast.

Each blow in itself wasn't enough to actually hurt her, but as he crisscrossed the whip marks, it sent a jolt through her body. She stopped counting at the twentieth blow, her body going into overload as he landed a direct hit against her pussy.

Screaming softly, she arched against the bed, instinctively wiggling away, which earned her several rapid blows against her tender core.

"Gregory,' she gasped, knowing she didn't really want him to stop.

The flail of the whip stopped, as he waited. When she didn't say anything else, he leaned down and pressed a kiss against her lips. After he moved back, she could hear him rustling in the drawer again, and knew she would be punished. He allowed her to moan and whimper, scream and wail at will, but she was only supposed to speak when he gave her leave, or when she truly couldn't take it any more.

He didn't want her to feel the need for a safe-word. He had explained simply that it was because if fear ever set in, she might not remember it. Instead, slowly he had trained her to speak only when in distress. For her to have spoken now, even something so simple as his name, while their emotions were running so high, was something she really shouldn't have done. She knew in her heart than Gregory would never hurt her, but he would push her to the edge of her sexual limits, drawing out her orgasm until she was ready to scream and beg for it.

A hum filled the stillness of the air as he turned on one of her vibrators. Trying to tell just which one by the sound was impossible, she had too many. Feeling the tip being pressed against her lips, she parted them and deep throated the mock cock, her pussy weeping for it to be moved there. And Gregory knew it …

Sucking on the dildo, she pretended it was his cock she was giving head to, running her tongue over the vein along the underside and swirling it around the tip. As Gregory pulled it free of her mouth with a faint pop, she trembled in anticipation.

He stroked it lightly over the tips of her nipples, driving her crazy. Oh so very slowly he moved the buzzing dildo down her body, trailing it over the ribs and into the valley of her belly button, before rubbing it with aching precision over her clit. He knew just how to draw it out, so that pleasure became almost pain as her body throbbed for more. He played her like a virtuoso would a fine instrument, with precision and sheer passion.

Without any warning, he pressed the dildo against her pouting pussy lips and thrust hard between them, sliding the fake cock halfway into her pussy. Melissa gasped and arched as the remainder of the eight inches was driven into her core.

Her pussy clenched around the plastic device, gasping at it in a vain effort to orgasm. Helpless, she couldn't do anything to push herself over the brink that Gregory kept her poised on. Everything was his call to make, her orgasm held to his whim. And she wouldn't have it any other way. She willing submitted to him, knowing he would provide what she needed to experience the height of pleasure.

She faintly could hear the rasp of his zipper and the subtle slide of material. When the bed dipped next to her head, she knew what was coming even before he straddled her and pressed his cock-head against her lips.

Sucking gently on the tip, she fought the instinctive gag as he thrust down into her throat. Tipping her head back, Melissa attained the perfect position to let him fuck her mouth. All that was required of her was her to suck and lick, as he thrust in and out. Tied as she was, she couldn't even palm his balls, or stroke his cock as she gave him head.

The slide of the dildo, infinitely slowly in and out was at drastic odds with the almost animalistic pump of his hips as he used her mouth to his will. The dildo jerked upwards, slamming against her pelvic bone as he gave a soft groan. Raking him with her teeth, she drew another groan from him.

"That's good baby. So very fucking good."

He dropped over her, his clothing brushing and torturing her clamped nipples and sensitive skin. Nuzzling at her small patch of hair, he started lapping at her clit, before removing the clamp with his teeth. Melissa gasped around his cock as the flow of blood returned with a sharp sting.

The pace of the dildo picked up, and even with her head held almost completely immobile, she knew what to do. Sucking at hard as she could, she stroked her tongue up and down his cock as he worked the plastic cock in and out of her pussy.

She could feel the familiar pull of her orgasm, but pushed it back with everything in her. To orgasm before him would ruin everything. Early in their relationship, she had gotten away with it. But now she had control over her climax, and knew how much it pleased him to command her when to come.

Arching into his mouth, she thrilled as he ground his face down, his tongue tracing the edge of her pussy, which was stretched by the girth of the dildo. His cock throbbed in her mouth, and then a warm jet gushed out, followed by a second, then a third. Gregory groaned against her pussy, his teeth clamping down on her clit.

Whimpering at the sensation, Melissa fought back the pounding rush of her orgasm, waiting for those precious words to leave his mouth. Melissa licked at the corner of her mouth, savoring the tiny trail of his semen as he pulled his cock from her mouth.

Gregory gasped for breath, and she thrilled as always at the beautiful sound.

The steady motions of the dildo stopped and she almost screamed in frustration. Then she felt the tightness on her ankles give as Gregory untied them.

The bed dipped as Gregory shifted on it, moving to untie her wrists from the headboard. With a soft touch, he repositioned them both, so that she was leaning back into his body while he leaned against the headboard.

It was how they often cuddled together to watch TV at night. It was almost surreal to lay in the same position as he started the thrusts of the dildo into her pussy again. Her nerves tingled throughout her body, as the blood rushed to her skin. She could feel the blush of need covering her body, and it took everything she had to hold back the urge to beg for an orgasm. Gregory still hadn't given her permission to speak, but neither had he given her permission to orgasm either.

His lips pressed tender kisses against her neck, in stark contrast to the deep thrusts of the fake cock in her pussy. Tender and fierce at once, it was enough to send her senses to a whole new level. Time seemed to slow, each moment a beat of her heart, as she waited in limbo for hr lover to give his permission. Lost in the sensations coursing through her body, she came to a startling realization. She was going to marry Gregory.

"You did wonderful baby."

His whispered praise against the tender skin of her neck was the most precious thing she had ever heard. He wasn't the most talkative of men, but when he spoke she knew he meant what he said.

"Now come for me baby."

His permission secured, she stopped fighting the rush of sensations that had hammered at her body, and let her mind float in the ecstasy flooding her system. Closing her eyes behind the blindfold, she worked to keep her breathing steady, and fought the urge to hold her breath as he started pumping the dildo into her pussy with a renewed vigor, even as he pinched her stinging nipples.

With a rush, her orgasm washed over her, sending her spiraling out of control. Screaming out her enjoyment, her love and passion for him, Melissa came apart for Gregory.

Jerking in his arms, she trembled and thrashed, euphoria sweetly filling her body and blocking everything else out.

When she opened her eyes, the blindfold was gone and Gregory was naked beside her, his fingers gently stroking through her sweat-dampened auburn hair.

"Welcome back," he whispered, then pressed a soft kiss against her lips. She lifted her bound arms and wrapped them around his neck, holding him tight against her. Rather than protest, he leaned into her touch, letting them both savor the affection that flowed between them.

Looking into his brown eyes, she could see the faintest hints of hurt still lingering, and it broke her heart that she had brought him anything but pleasure.

"Yes Gregory, yes I will marry you."

His lips curled in a smile moments before he clasped her against him and climbed from the bed. Spinning her around in a circle, he laughed with sheer joy, the sound so very sweet to her ears.

It was true, there was the chance she could one day regret marrying him. Life never offered any certainties. But the chance of future unhappiness was overshadowed by the certainty that if she didn't marry him, she would definitely regret it. She just had to trust that what they had would last.

* * *

TIED WITH A BOW

Sylvia lit the last candle on the nightstand and laid down the lighter. She picked up her list and pen, crossing the second to last item off. Muttering to herself, she went over the list again, just to double check things. "Purchase jingle bells, mistletoe, and red ribbons, check. Change the sheets and make the bed, check. Take a nice long bath with lots of bubbles, check. Change into naughty Ms. Claus nightgown with added accessories, check. All that's left is the soft, slow Christmas music and I'm all set."

Humming *White Christmas*, she tossed the list in the trash and crossed the room to the dresser where the CD player sat silent. She had no sooner turned it on when the front door opened. It only took a moment, so she flipped her head down and tousled her sandy tresses, giving the appearance of having just had wild sex. She knew Devin loved seeing her hair in wild disarray almost as much as he enjoyed the sight of her kneeling before him, her lips wrapped around his cock.

"Sylvia? Honey, where are you?" Devin called out. Sylvia could hear him flicking the light switch, but since she had removed the bulbs earlier, she knew it wasn't going to do him much good.

"In the bedroom, dear," she called back, giving a little shimmy to settle her nightgown and robe. The tinkling of bells accompanied her movements.

"What happened to the lights?" She could hear her husband moving down the hall, the soles of his shoes loud on the hardwood floor. Luckily, the Christmas tree in the living room, with its twinkling lights, would provide enough illumination for him to make his way safely down the hall.

Casting one last glance about the room, from the soft sheets to the flicker of candlelight against the walls, she made sure everything was perfect. "I unscrewed them."

As his steps brought him closer, she reached down and picked up the velvet robe she'd bought him for Valentine's Day, which he hadn't worn since.

"Now, why on earth did you..." his voice trailed off as he entered the room and saw her standing there.

Walking slowly across the room, she swayed her hips slightly, with just enough jiggle to get her breasts bouncing and her bells jingling. "Welcome home baby. Merry Christmas."

After setting his robe at her feet, she gave him a quick kiss and began removing his scrubs. The shirt tried to cling to his skin, moist with sweat, but she gave it a not so gentle tug and succeeded in pulling it over his head. She had just started to undo the tie at his waist when he shook himself out of his stupor. "Sylvia, baby, let me do that. I'm all sweaty and I know I must smell awful."

Despite his hands covering hers, she continued fidgeting with his drawstring until it came undone. She pushed his pants and boxers down his hips and sank to her knees in front of him, the fake fur trim of her nightie brushing her upper thighs.

Devin dutifully stepped out of his pants as she tugged first one leg then the other. She tossed the last of his clothing aside, leaned forward and nuzzled against his stomach, rubbing her face against the faint pleasure trail of blonde hair leading down to his groin. She looked up and met his blue-eyed gaze. "I missed you baby," she said, placing tiny kisses along his abs. "Next year, tell them you're not working Christmas Eve."

"Ah honey, you know I would've loved to have been here."

"I know." Nipping at his stomach, she stifled a grin at his surprised yelp. "But I'm glad you're here now."

Without any warning, she shifted down, taking his cock-head into her mouth. Sucking at his soft flesh, she slowly worked up and down his length while his hands fisted in her still damp hair. Just as he grew hard in her mouth, she pulled back and sat on her heels. "Go take a quick shower. I'll be waiting."

"Tease."

"No baby, not a tease, just a taste of what's to come." Picking up the robe where it lay beside her, she handed it to him and held out her hand. After he had pulled her to her feet, she turned and crossed to the bed, the bells on her outfit jingling with each step. "Now hurry up."

She reclined on the bed, her breasts thrust out, straining against the tight faux velvet of her outfit. Devin took a step toward her. With a soft chuckle, Sylvia shooed him away. "Go get your shower."

As soon as the bathroom door closed, she climbed off the bed and hurried to the dresser. Changing the CD to slow Christmas jazz, she turned the volume down low. She was pulling the top sheet down to the foot of the bed when she heard the shower turn on. Humming beneath her breath, she quickly tied pre-cut strips of red ribbon to each of the four bedposts. The last one done, she climbed back on to the bed, just as the shower shut off.

Moments later, Devin returned, his robe on and belted, toweling his hair dry.

"Baby, you look so damn sexy." The husky tone to Devin's voice made her heart race. She knew he would have found her attractive dressed in a potato sack, but it was nice to see the heat flare in his blue eyes as his gaze trailed over her, darkening them to a navy. Slowly she opened her fur-trimmed robe and shrugged it from her shoulders. As it slid down her back, she took a deep breath which thrust her breasts against her nightgown.

With the robe pooled around her hips, she reclined against the pillows and patted the bed next to her. She almost couldn't breathe, she was so excited about her plans.

Devin climbed on the bed and settled beside her, leaning down to engage her in a kiss. Tongues dueling, she gently guided him onto his back and leaned over him.

Clasping one of his hands in hers, she pulled his arm over his head, his wrist pressed against the bedpost. Quickly, she tied a loose knot on the ribbon, binding him. After sweeping her robe from the bed, she repeated the process on his other wrist before turning around, and tying one of his feet. Her butt, bare except for the thong between her cheeks, wiggled as she worked, earning her a groan from her husband.

"Why don't you scoot that luscious ass of yours back about a foot?"

Sylvia leaned to the side and tipped her head, so that Devin could see her face. Pursing her lips, she blew him a kiss then returned to the task of tying his other ankle to the bed's remaining post.

Job done, she slid off the bed and stood beside him, admiring her husband, tied spread eagle on the bed. "Comfortable?" she asked.

"Mmm, except for the fact that right before my shower, some little vixen sucked my cock hard, then stopped." Sylvia trailed her gaze down her husband's velvet clad body, to the tent his cock made.

"We'll have to make sure she's spanked later then, but for now, she wants to play." Sylvia reached out and untied the robe's belt, then slipped the flaps to the side, freeing his cock from the weight of the velvet. Teasing him, she ran her fingertips lightly up and down the length, circling around the head, then back down to his balls. Cupping them in her palm, she rolled them gently in her hand, as Devin arched his hips. Gently, she stroked a fingertip against his anus as she massaged his balls.

"Have you been a good boy this year?"

Devin rolled his eyes at her, then answered, "Yes ma'am. But my wife hasn't. She's a little *tease*!" He raised his voice slightly on the last word. Sylvia wasn't sure if it was on purpose or because she had slipped her fingertip into his ass, but if she had to guess, she'd say it was because of her.

"Poor little boy. Your wife sounds like such a naughty girl." As she spoke, Sylvia climbed onto the bed and straddled Devin's chest, the fur trim of her nightgown brushing against his chin.

"Oh ma'am, she is. She's *such* a naughty girl, but I love her."

"Mmm, that's good. Would you like to open one of your presents now, since you're being such a good boy?"

Devin's eyes twinkled. "Oh definitely."

Sylvia lifted the edge of her nightgown, showing off her red and white lace thong. Shifting forward, she raised up on her knees and dangled one of the two ties that held it closed against his lips. Devin caught on quick. Tipping his head to the side, he caught the tie in his teeth and pulled.

As soon as he let go, Sylvia shifted and they repeated the process. The moment Devin let the other tie go, the thong parted and fell, pooling on his chest. His eyes widened as his gaze locked on her pussy.

She knew he was staring at the tiny red ribbon she had tied around the clip attached to her clit, and the matching ones that dangled from her pussy lips and ass-bud."

"Guess where I hid the jingle bells?" His eyes widened further than she dreamed possible as a truly wicked grin lit up his face.

"Inside one of my presents?"

"Uh-huh. But first, you have another one to unwrap."

Careful not to press too hard on his shoulders, she slid forward, positioning her pussy a breath away from his lips. As his tongue moistened his lips, he inadvertently teased her already throbbing clit.

Moaning softly, she ground down on his mouth, pressing his warm, wet tongue against her needy flesh. Almost ravenously, he dived in, swirling his tongue around her pulsing clit, sucking the tiny bud into his mouth, his teeth clinking against the metal of her clitoris clamp.

"Quit teasing," she panted, "and open your present."

Luckily for her sanity, he did, catching one end of the bow in his teeth. Sylvia lifted slightly, whimpering at the pleasure-pain as the ribbon pulled on the metal loop around her clit, before slipping it free of her flesh.

Reaching down, she stroked her fingers around her clit, playing with the throbbing pearl. Devin's gaze followed her every movement, as right before his eyes, juices dripped from her quivering core.

Thighs quivering, she leaned forward, brushing the ribbon that dangled from her pussy against his lips. Nipping the ribbon, he caught hold, and Sylvia pulled back slowly. The first bell slipped past her lips with a muted pop, the ribbon soaked with her essence. Trembling slightly, she shifted back, as another bell, and another slipped free. She had gotten the idea from the anal beads she and Devin played with all the time, and it had taken almost a week of trial and error to find jingle bells just the right size. Another couple of days were devoted to finding a way to coat them so their rough edges wouldn't tear her skin as they were pulled free.

As the eleventh bell slipped free, she pinched her clit and kept moving back, her inner muscles clenching tight. Sylvia knew the last one would send her over the edge. Breath held, she leaned back as the last bell, by far the largest, pulling against the inside of her lips, rubbing against enflamed flesh. Whimpering, she dropped backwards, her knees bent, and the last bell slipped free, sending her orgasm crashing down on her. Manipulating her clit, she rode the waves, prolonging her enjoyment, while Devin whispered nonsense words to her. He might have been saying something important, but she couldn't tell--a dull roar filled her ears

Once reason returned, she sat up. Devin met her gaze, a grin on his face. "Feeling better, babe?"

"Mmmm, yeah," she knew she sounded dopey, but she felt so good. With his hectic schedule, she and Devin hadn't enjoyed more than the most fleeting of intimate moments in about six months. She also hadn't masturbated in the last three weeks, in anticipating of Christmas. She wasn't certain how she was going to survive the rest of his residency, but wasn't going to dwell on it now.

Wiggling slightly, she set the bells on her outfit to jingling again as she shifted around, until her pussy pressed against his cock.

"I do have to admit, that was erotic as hell," he said, his voice strained as she reached between them and slipped his cock-head past her pussy lips. Lifting up, she positioned him solidly; she slid back down, as he raised his hips, thrusting his cock up and into her core.

"Mmm hhhm," she murmured, his cock pressing against the sensitive inner walls of her pussy.

Rocking back and forth as he thrust up against her, they settled into a slow and steady rhythm. "I definitely enjoyed it."

Her smile wicked, Sylvia reached up and untied the top of her nightgown, letting the halter strap slip down, baring her breasts. She had also tied tiny red ribbons through her nipple rings. One ribbon attached to both rings, with another joined with it at its middle, it formed a festive Y, with another bell at the end.

She pushed the nightgown down further so that it bunched at her waist, even while she continued to grind against her husband, his curly black pubic hairs tickling her clit.

"Want to play with your last present?"

Devin nodded.

Careful not to pull too tight, Sylvia caught the ribbon as it dangled between then, and pressed the bell on the end against Devin's lips. He pursed them, holding the bell between them, but not trapping it.

Sylvia leaned back slightly, her breasts jiggling as she rocked harder against him. The ribbon stretched taut, pulling on her nipple rings.

Whimpering as the pain sent sparks of pleasure throughout her body, Sylvia clenched her pussy tight, milking Devin's cock as she worked up and down, pushing them both closer to a shared orgasm.

With each thrust, Devin tipped his head back, giving a tiny pull to the ribbon. Sylvia couldn't have planned it better. Her nipples stretched and tingled with each tiny tug.

She could feel the familiar twitching of her core, heralding what was to come. Reaching a hand behind her, she gripped the last remaining ribbon, and gently pulled. The first bell slipped from her ass with a well-lubricated pop.

"Oh," she gasped. Leaning a bit forward, she tugged again, and a second bell slipped free. "More. Devin, more."

The bed creaked as he picked up his pace, thrusting as hard upward as his bonds would allow him. His breath matched hers, fast and hard, almost gasping as they both raced to the finish line.

Another tug and a third bell slipped free. Sylvia fought the urge to bite her lip at the familiar sting. Her asshole was on fire.

She clenched her pussy muscles tight, as she gave a not so gentle tug and the last bell strained free. Tipping back, even as the bell dropped to the bed, she tightened the slack on the ribbon attached to her nipples. Screaming at the triple pleasure, she trembled in euphoria as she climaxed.

Beneath her, Devin grunted, his motions tiny jerks, as he joined her.

Collapsing against his chest, Sylvia moaned softly as hot jets of his cream flooded her core. Both struggled to catch their breath while at the same time prolonging their pleasure. Sylvia wiggled slightly, grinding Devin's pubic hair against her clit, sending lingering tingles throughout her pussy.

As soon as she could move again, Sylvia reached up and untied his arms. Flopping back against his chest, she cuddled close. His arms wrapped around her, holding her close.

"Damn baby, I have to admit, that was a great Christmas present."

Snuggling closer, Sylvia murmured her agreement.

"Although I do have to wonder two things. One, what do you have in mind for New Year's Eve? And two, are you planning to untie my feet anytime soon?"

Grumbling good naturedly, Sylvia sat up and stripped off her nightgown, then attended to his remaining bonds, while he slipped off the robe and tossed it to the other side of the bedroom.

As they settled back into each other's arms, Devin tried again. "So what's planned for New Year's Eve?"

Sylvia just grinned, thinking about the bag she had hidden under the kitchen sink.

* * *

A PASSION FOR LEARNING

Arianna leaned against the counter and pursed her lips. Tracing the pouting lines with a layer of gloss, she pressed them together and leaned back. Finally satisfied at her appearance, she headed towards the basement where her husband waited for their newest game. Although she knew her part, she wasn't quite certain what awaited her.

Hurrying down the carpeted steps, she opened the door and stepped into a mock classroom.

"So nice of you to join us Ms. Bradford. Have a seat so we can get started."

Swaying her hips subtly, Arianna crossed the room and took the only seat available. Her pleated skirt barely covered her cheeks, and the tops of her thighs touched the cold wood of her desk chair, causing her to gasp as she sat down.

"Now class, last night's homework was to study the scientific method. Let's see who studied and who didn't." Moving to the chalkboard, he wrote a big number one.

"The first step is? Anyone? Anyone?"

Arianna slouched down in her seat, struggling to remember her old high school science. She knew what was coming, Neil had told her all about his fantasy.

"Ms. Bradford, how about you. What's the first stage of the scientific method?"

Blushing, Arianna stuttered, "Um sir, I don't know."

"Didn't you do your homework last night?"

Sliding further down into her chair, Arianna shook her head. As Neil turned and walked behind his desk, she could feel her pussy quivering with anticipation. This was it; this was the beginning of the fantasy.

"Come here Ms. Bradford. Class, the rest of you are dismissed." Grinning since no one else was actually in the room, Arianna almost giggled at his words until she saw what he pulled from his desk drawer. Twelve inches long, the paddle reminded her of ones in books about corporal punishment, back when that was allowed in schools. Reaching into his desk drawer again, he pulled out a wooden ruler. Soon a switch and a belt joined the pile on his desk.

Stepping around to the side of his desk, he waited, his hand caressing the leather of his belt.

"Um, Nnn, um sir, I," she whispered, hesitating a few steps away. Uncertainty warred with need.

"Now, Ms. Bradford," he barked, stepping to the edge of his desk.

She gasped as he pushed her down over it.

"I'm tired of your lack of attention to your school work. Your parents pay good money for your education, and you're throwing it all away."

Keeping his hand in the small of her back, he pushed down harder, the hard wood of the desk digging into her tender breasts. Nipples erect with desire, Arianna wiggled slightly trying to ease the pressure.

"I think it is time for us to go over last night's lesson. The first stage of the scientific method is identifying the problem." He paused.

Arianna caught her breath in anticipation.

"Now, as I see it, we have two problems: How to make learning fun, and how to punish you for not doing as you are told."

His hand on her back, he flipped the tiny skirt up, baring her milky white cheeks, with a thong string between them. Pulling it away from her flesh, he snapped the thong bikini's string and slipped the torn material from her body.

"You can't do this to me."

Neil responded by pressing down harder against her back. Raising his other hand, he smacked Arianna's tender ass, a red handprint springing to life.

"Ouch! You can't do this!" she squealed.

"Mmmm, yes I can. You see Ms. Bradford, you parents are fed up with your antics; staying out late with boys, skipping classes, failing grades. They've given me leave to do as I will to improve your learning. Now, repeat after me, the first stage is to identify the problem."

Pressing her lips together, Arianna refused to say what he ordered. Several moments passed in silence.

Smack!

"Ouch!" Arianna wailed. Clenching her legs together, she struggled to focus on the pain and not the delicious tingle working its way throughout her body. She needed this. She needed to give Neil their fantasy, to prolong every naughty moment.

"Say it."

"No."

Again his hand smacked her flesh, rosy with his attention.

Moaning softly, she whispered what he demanded.

"Good. Now, the second stage is to hypothesize the result. The problem as stated is your lack of attention to schoolwork. I hypothesize that by the time we're done here today, I will have found a way to focus your attention on your lessons.

"Now Ms. Bradford, I think for our second stage a belt is appropriate."

She could see out of the corner of her eye as Neil grasped the smooth leather, gripping the buckle in his fist. Snapping it lightly in the air, he snapped it again, this time blazing a fiery path on Arianna's bottom.

"Ow, shit!" she yelped.

"Such language will not be tolerated." Snapping the belt again, he crisscrossed his earlier line, creating a stinging x across her ass.

"Ohhh, sorry sir," she whimpered. Her pussy clenched with the need for his cock, but still she held back. Her ass already on fire, she couldn't imagine it getting any better.

"Repeat the second stage."

"To form a hypothesis, sir."

Gently he stroked his hand over her cheeks, with his other hand pressed firmly against her spine. "Good. The third stage is to create a procedure, a plan of action, and to experiment. Just like now I plan to experiment with the paddle. I think you'll like this one, Ms. Bradford. It will cover so much territory and make it hurt all that much more."

She turned her head and watched as he set the belt aside, and firmly grasped the paddle. She could hear a faint whistle of air followed by a solid crack as it connected with her ass. The dull thud of it hitting her flesh was misleading, giving the impression that it wasn't going to hurt. Arianna relaxed as the paddle pulled away, only to have an intense spark of pain radiate throughout her cheeks as the delayed reaction kicked in. Her ass-ring clenched in anticipation as Neil swung again. This time, she was prepared for the exquisite pleasure-pain the paddle wrought.

"Ohhh," she whimpered, her juices trickling down her inner thighs, adding a glossy sheen to her creamy skin.

"Yes Ms. Bradford, I think that was lovely too. Now say it."

"Plan and experiment."

"Good. Now for stage four." Again he selected another object to experiment with. "Let's try the switch this time. This might sting a little more Ms. Bradford, but remember this is for your own good. Four is to organize and analyze your data."

With a hollow whistle, the switch landed against her ass.

"*OUCH!*" she gasped. Wiggling, she struggled to move out from under his hand.

"We must always try something more than once before we decide that we don't like it." Neil rained a light blow to her pussy. "Sometimes we have to repeat our experiment before we can move on to step five."

Arianna sucked in a quick breath at the unexpected contact. "Sometimes Ms. Bradford, things don't always go as planned. Now I think that was unexpected. Let's try it again, shall we?"

Another hollow whistle and the switch landed against her pouting nether lips.

"Ummm," she whimpered, her hips arching back for more.

"Interesting. Definitely unexpected, Ms. Bradford. Stage four is all about our data, analyzing it. But since I'm busy, you'll have to do it for me. What have we observed so far?"

Fighting the urge to beg for his cock, Arianna struggled to put to words what he wanted.

"Stage one is to identify the problem."

"No, no, no," Neil returned, tapping her pussy lightly with each word. "Don't tell me the stages; tell me the results of our experiment."

"Oh, um," pausing to lick her lips, Arianna began again, "I um, liked the paddle and your hand, but the belt hurt. The switch is nice against my pussy, but not my ass, and there is one more stage to go, as well as one more object to experiment with, sir."

"Very good Ms. Bradford, I think you are learning quickly. After our lesson, we'll have to see about some extra credit work to make up on your lost assignments. I think you could easily become an A student."

She trembled as he gently stroked his hand over her ass. "The last stage is to draw a conclusion and communicate our results. So, let's draw our conclusion, shall we?"

"Yes," she whispered, breathless with anticipation. She knew what was coming–the wooden ruler, the last object to try. *As for his other plans, he had better intend to fuck me senseless soon,* she thought.

"Now, what's the last stage?"

"The conclusion, sir."

"Very good." A sharp whistle followed by a delicious sting. Gasping, Arianna trembled. Her spine arched, his hand unconsciously popping her back.

Again he smacked the ruler against her ass. A zing of pleasure accompanied the swat, racing from her pussy to her nipples.

"Oh yesss," she moaned. Collapsing against the desk, she enjoyed the rapture of his remaining three swats.

She knew by now her cheeks must be a bright shade of red. She resisted the urge to step out of character and rush to the bathroom to see them firsthand. She had a feeling they looked delicious against her creamy skin.

"Yes Ms. Bradford, I think this has gone very well." Removing his hand, Neil moved over to his chair and collapsed in it. Quickly unzipping his slacks, he pulled his cock free. Arianna almost wept in relief; he was finally ready to fuck. She was more than ready, had been from the first smack of his hand.

"Come here Ms. Bradford. I want to examine the result of our experiment, to make sure all of the variables have been sampled."

Her legs trembling, Arianna stood up and slowly moved around the desk. She had a very good idea what a newborn foal felt like, trying to take its first steps. Every flex of her ass as she walked rekindled a trail of fiery pain along her cheeks.

Standing before him, Arianna bent over, baring her ass and, indirectly, her dripping pussy to his view. Neil slipped a finger between her wet lips. Arianna could feel her juices leaking down her thighs. She couldn't believe she held out as long as she had; every nerve in her body was screaming for more.

She moaned and swished her hips as she sought to drive his thrusting finger deeper.

"Uh uh, Ms. Bradford, I have other plans for you. Open my desk drawer."

Regretfully, Arianna pulled away from his finger and stood up. Sliding the drawer open, she saw only one remaining object, a plastic graduated cylinder with the base filed down so that it was as smooth and rounded as the bottom of a test tube.

Cocking an eyebrow at him, Arianna asked a silent question. "That's right Ms. Bradford, pick it up and hand it to me."

Tentatively, she clasped the 100ml tube, her hand trembling from excitement. This was beyond what she had ever imagined, yet it felt right and deliciously kinky all at once.

"Give it to me," he demanded again, steel lacing his words. Looking down at his cock, Arianna could see why. His head was a deep angry red, about the color she imagined her ass to be.

Placing the cylinder in his hand, she waited for his next command. It wasn't long in coming. "Hop onto the desk. That's good. Now part your legs for me. Yes, such a good pupil now aren't you? I think I've discovered the secret. Be a good girl and part those pretty pussy lips for me. I need to test one more thing before my conclusion will be complete, and the extra credit will do you good."

Bracing her weight on her arms, Arianna half reclined, half sat on the desk, her legs dangling from the edge. Her pussy was spread before Neil, smooth shaven and glistening with her arousal.

Gripping the cylinder so tightly his knuckles showed white, Neil pressed the rounded tip against her opening and lightly pushed. With a wet pop, it slipped in. Thrusting halfway in, he stroked his cock with his other hand as Arianna collapsed onto the desk, watching his fist work up and down his hard length.

Whimpering and arching into the mock dildo, she ground against his palm, sweet release within her grasp. She barely registered him pressing a finger against her ass-ring, or it slipping inside. Her insides turned to jello as Neil subtly lubed her ass, while thrusting the pseudo-dildo in and out of her pussy, teasing her by changing the pace, the raised lines that marked each measurement scraping against her slick inner walls. Sweet anticipation flooded her pussy with each thrust and retreat.

Curling her nails into her palms, Arianna felt tears of frustration spring to her eyes.

"Oh yes, sir," she begged, "please? I promise to do better, to listen in class and to do my homework. Please sir?"

After pulling the cylinder from her quivering pussy, he quickly pressed it against her ass-ring and pushed. Wet with her juices and her bodies' lubrication, it slipped in with little resistance and the ridges along the side caused it to stay.

Panting with lust, Arianna pleaded for him to fuck her.

"Come here Ms. Bradford, it's time for that extra special credit." The graduated cylinder sticking obscenely from her ass, Arianna climbed off the desk and straddled his lap, his cock rubbing against her pussy in a sinfully delicious way.

"That's it Ms. Bradford, slide down on my cock like a good girl."

While impaling herself on his cock, Arianna reached behind her and manipulated the cylinder in and out of her ass as she bounced up and down on his lap. The chair creaked under the weight and force of their motions, but she didn't care and doubted that Neil did either. They were lost in a world of fantasy and passion, of classroom discipline and the taboo. He was the teacher, she the student and physics was irrelevant to them both.

All that mattered was the steady thrust of his cock within her forbidden pussy.

"Yes Ms. Bradford," Neil groaned, his voice tight, "fuck my cock like the naughty girl you are. Tell me, I have to know; what was so important last night that you didn't do your homework?"

Her pussy quivering with need, Arianna gasped as the first ripples of her orgasm built.

"I was sucking my boyfriend off," she panted, "letting him come all over my breasts and face. Then, oh god sir, yes like that, oh yeah then I let him eat my pussy until I came."

Arianna clenched her inner muscles tight as Neil jerked within her, his orgasm a catalyst to her own. Squealing her delight at the sticky warmth that invaded her body, Arianna orgasmed. Her body limp, she collapsed against his chest, and rocked slowly up and down, her body unconsciously driving towards another, smaller orgasm.

As she quivered with the lingering traces of euphoria, Neil reached down and slipped the pseudo-dildo from her tender ass.

"Mmmm, so tell me Neil, what conclusion did you reach?"

Chuckling, he wrapped his arms around her and cuddled her against his chest.

"Well Arianna I think you liked it. Makes me wonder about another fantasy of mine. See, there is this patient that comes to me. She's about to get married and needs her prenuptial check up. I of course, being the concerned doctor ..."

ALSO AVAILABLE

If you enjoyed Kinky Girls Do, you might also enjoy …

A Second Chance at Love

MICHELLE HOUSTON

The first time around they weren't ready. Now five star-crossed couples get …

A SECOND CHANCE AT Love

"a sexy read of love and trust"
~ Sensual Reads and Reviews

978-0692251157

The first time around, they weren't ready. Now five star-crossed couples get A Second Chance at Love.

DIGGIN' UP BONES:

Zach's back - and he's digging for answers …
All Alisa wants is to be left alone, but the discovery of Native American bones on her property make that wish

impossible. Zach Bradford's back in her life, bringing a whole lot of memories she wants to forget and questions she doesn't want to answer. He's not just digging for bones, he's digging into their past, searching for answers. Now Alisa must decide if she wants to live in the past or reach for a future with Zach.

A BID FOR LOVE:

He bought her for 48 hours ...
Erika thought Ryan was out of her life. She thought she was over him. When he outbids her at an auction on her grandmother's painting, she's willing to do anything to get it from him. Her head says she can walk away after 48 hours. Her heart isn't so sure.

WILLED TO LOVE:

Two former lovers are unprepared for the reading of a will. Can they live up to the terms?
Ashley Monroe wants a divorce. Not because she doesn't love her husband, but because she can't take his family's mistreatment any longer. Devon's grandmother isn't about to let history repeat itself; she wrote her will to make sure of it.

A CHANGE OF PACE:

Ten years ago, they were students in the same college class - but Nicole never imagined Alan saw her as anything more than a study-buddy. Now that's about to change ...
Nicole is frustrated with the emptiness of her life. A chance meeting with an old classmate ends with an invitation to his house for dinner. Nicole has enough regrets about the past. She's not about to pass up what might be a second chance.

HER BEST MAN:

What if her love for Rick wasn't unrequited?
Rick's always been part of Katherine's life. He was even her husband's best man at their wedding. And secretly, she's always had more feelings for her husband's best man than she should have. When her marriage falls apart, she finds out she's not the only one who's been keeping feelings secret.

AUTHOR'S NOTE

There is a difference between consensual D/s and out-and
-out abuse. In D/s, the submissive partner can call a halt -
without repercussions.

If you find yourself in an abusive situation, there are
resources available to you - both local and national. In the
US, some of the national resources are:

The Joyful Heart Foundation
http://www.joyfulheartfoundation.org/

The National Domestic Violence Hotline
http://www.thehotline.org/

The National Coalition Against Domestic Violence
http://www.ncadv.org/

Any of these national services can coordination your
contact with a local facility.

* * *

ABOUT THE AUTHOR

Born to ride on the back of dragons, to journey among the stars in a ship traveling faster than light, or to dance the night away in the arms of a mysterious vampire, Michelle Houston willingly shares the worlds in her mind in an effort to bring them to life.

Writing everything from short and sweet stories, to hot and spicy tales of kink, from contemporary tales of erotic romance to erotica romances featuring Greek gods, vampires and were-creatures, she has crossed sexualities and has gone wherever her mental muse has guided her, a journey she has never regretted.

As for the more mundane details: Michelle is a Sagittarius, born in the Chinese zodiac Year of the Horse. She currently resides in the Midwest US with her husband and daughter. Michelle has a love of the natural world around us (except for insects, spiders, snakes, scorpions, and she reserves the right to add more at any time). She's one of those people that actually liked Biology in High School, and enjoys learning about all things science.

In other words, she is an ordinary woman with an imagination that is only held in bounds by how fast she can type.

You can find out more about Michelle Houston on her author website at: www.michellehouston.com